# FROM ICE
## AND SNOW

# FROM ICE AND SNOW

## A Fictional Memoir

LIFE IS CALLING – BOOK II

## Dianne Kozdrey Bunnell

Wordsmith Publishing

# AUTHOR'S NOTE

*From Ice and Snow* is a fictional memoir, the second book in the series, Life Is Calling, following Book 1, *The Protest*.

Both stories are inspired by a real-life incident. All of the characters are the product of my imagination, and their actions, motivations, thoughts, and conversations are solely my creation. I have drawn inspiration from my own experiences, but the characters, the situations in which they found themselves, as well as the locations, real and fictional, and the non-existent religious sect, The Fellowship of the Holy Bible and its minister and members, are not intended to depict real people, settings, or events.

If you'd like to know when I release future stories, please join my New Release Mailing List: *www.diannekbunnell.com*.

I won't send you any unnecessary emails and I will guard your privacy. In fact, I will only contact you when I have a new story to share with you. It's the very best way I have to stay in touch with my readers.

*For My Daughters*

# FROM ICE
## AND SNOW

# 1

"I think Lisa dumped me today," Simon Bernard said, not looking up from his plate at the dinner table.

"You've been together for what, a month now, maybe two? What makes you think she's dumped you?" his father asked.

"Well, she sent a text saying something about going to the movies with this guy who's in her astronomy class— he's on the rowing team and a big man at the U. Neither of them came home for the break." The twenty-year-old put his fork down, placed his chin in his palm, and sighed.

Bolivar Bernard chewed his food thoughtfully.

Jane Bernard imagined her husband was turning the seriousness of the situation over in his mind before answering. She glanced at Simon, who watched him. In her stepson's look, Jane saw hope, as if his father's wisdom would supply him with the perfect response to show the depth of his feelings for Lisa to win her back.

"Well, son," Bolivar said, "I can't say what will change a woman's heart—no man can do that. But think about this: maybe she's not interested because she's noticed you're getting kinda thin on top."

Simon exploded in laughter and Bo chuckled, casting a glance at the thick hair blanketing his son's head.

"Hope I'm not taking after you, Dad." Simon reached over and brushed his hand over his father's sparse hair.

Jane found herself smiling at the absurdity of her husband's remark, his giving up to comedy in the face of trying to understand women.

As she watched Simon relishing his father's off-the-wall humor, Jane's chest tightened. The sight of father and son so thoroughly at ease with each other, taking such delight in one another's company made the bile rise in her throat. *Damn it,* she thought, not over Bo's remark or Simon's enjoyment of it, but because it gave rise to thoughts of her daughters.

Jane Bernard had always believed in herself as a mother. Her strong natural confidence was influenced by the good mothering she had received as a child. A tender heart made the love of her daughters and stepson warm, understanding, unconditional. Yet, the softness was tempered by a firmness that never sacrificed her authority. She wore the mantle of motherhood easily.

Jane thought of Bekah and Darcy often. How could she not? Yet, now when she watched her husband and her stepson locked together by love, she couldn't help looking inside herself, where she found her mother's heart crouched amongst the bedlam left by the loss of her daughters.

*I can't stand it. The lawyer called it a Solomon-like decision. It killed me, it's still killing me. Why did I do it? Why?*

"I'm not hungry," she said, scraping her seat back from the dinner table. She strode toward the door.

Bo said quietly to his son, "You know it's not about you or me." Simon looked after Jane, nodding slowly.

She whirled and shot back, "You don't have to rub it in. You don't know what I'm going through. Simon's got his dad—and you've got your son. Sometimes I just get so fed up when I'm around you two. Seeing you having a good time together makes me sick. *You* try acting normal when all the sweetness has gone out of your life. I can't." She turned and left the room.

Bo locked eyes with Simon, then slowly pushed back from the table. He walked down the hallway and knocked quietly on the bedroom door. Receiving no response, he went in, closed the door behind him, and sat on the bed next to Jane.

She stared dully at the floor. He observed her reflection in the dark window. The long chestnut hair hung forward across her cheek, a screen of copper highlights in the lamp glow.

"I know it's hard for you sometimes and you're feeling bad," he said.

She heaved a sigh and shrugged.

"Jane, look at me."

She turned her back to him, recovered enough to feel embarrassed for her outburst.

Bolivar's voice was stern. "Look at me."

Jane's head jerked up and she turned to face him. The harsh voice commanding her attention was something new. Her pulse quickened. This did not sound like the gentle husband she knew. Still, it only inflamed her anger. Her unreasoning anger felt dangerous, strong, capable of ripping her away from the safe harbor of Bolivar's love.

It had reached for such annihilation in the dining room; now it made her tremble.

For years, she had allowed herself to wallow in the catastrophe that defined her lost motherhood. In the beginning, she naively reasoned that her sacrifice for the sake of her girls would be enough to keep her heart and mind from breaking, keep her outlook on life from turning bitter. She had let her girls go to live with their father and his wife to save their brain-washed minds. Logan Churlick, their father, was waging war against Jane. Her girls were being poisoned against her and torn apart psychologically. She could never let that happen. Letting them go, in order to save them, was the hardest thing she had ever done. And Bo had stood by her over the years, loving and patient.

"I'd say I'm sorry—but I don't feel sorry," Jane said, her sharp look strange in its intensity. "It felt good to just let it fly."

Bo nodded, but his manner had lost its sympathy. "I'll bet. Did you think about how Simon might've taken it?"

She said nothing.

"I know you're suffering. You're not yourself. Times like this, you go to someplace inside and can't see . . ."

"Oh, I see." The words came from a dead place inside that chilled her heart.

She couldn't stop herself. Voice breaking, she said, "I see very well. We come into this world alone, and we leave this world alone. It's the way life is. I feel completely alone. Got it? We're not supposed to need anyone. And I don't. Not my girls, not Simon, not you."

Jane saw the pain in Bolivar's eyes, saw that he didn't understand. She felt reassurance in her self-imposed isolation and yet alarmed beyond all reason. She turned away from Bo and lay down on the bed. When she heard him retreat from the room, she let out a shuddering breath, not aware she had been holding it.

⁂

*Jane stood alone in the middle of a snowy clearing in the forest. She gathered her coat at her neck, struggling to walk through a blizzard. Odd-shaped lumps filled the clearing, tops rounded softly with snow. She had a strange feeling about the lumps and was drawn to them. But as she got close, she saw two figures, small and straight, fighting through the snow toward her. The moonlight glistened on them and Jane squinted against the gusts. As the figures moved closer, the fierce snow coated them. The crust grew thicker and thicker. Instinctively, she ran to help them. She heard their voices over the freezing blast of the wind. Maaah! Maaaw! The voices seized her heart. Bekah and Darcy. By the time she reached them, their faces and bodies were frozen inside hard, crusted ice capsules. She caressed them, wept over them, ranted and clawed at the ice, smashed it with her fists until she was bloody.*

Jane awoke sobbing. In the familiar nightmare, she never dreamed of the twins as the teens they were, but rather as twelve-year-olds, the age she'd lost them. Bo sat up in bed and pulled her to him, and she let herself be pulled. He held her as he always did, and she tried to extricate herself out of the great choking pain.

In the morning, Jane moved as if drugged by the dark ripples of the nightmare. In the steamy bathroom, she rubbed the mirror with a towel and stared at herself.

"I look like hell," she said, more curious than alarmed by the sight. She picked up a brush and pulled it through her wet hair.

Her thoughts migrated to the day ahead. *Gotta get those hand-outs copied before first period.* The arm holding the brush slowly came to rest on the sink. She thought of the students she loved teaching. She had a special plan in mind for her seniors, who were reading *The Grapes of Wrath.*

A jolt of hope and fear shot through her, and her hands flew to her mouth, palms together. She squeezed her eyes shut.

*It's April 9*, she thought, pulse quickening. *The twins'll be eighteen today. They'll be of age. Will Bekah and Darcy think of me on their eighteenth birthday?*

❧

Bekah looked over her shoulder. Her parents' bedroom was quiet, the only noise coming from downstairs in the kitchen where her sister was with Dolores, their adoptive mother. Her father, Reverend Logan Churlick, had already left for church. She reached into the large basket filled with parishioners' offerings on her father's dresser.

She fished out several bills. *That should be enough. He'll never notice out of all this cash.*

The money was to buy some marijuana from a friend. She thought about snatching some alcohol, but there was none in the house. *Not even wine*, she thought, *even though Jesus made it from water.*

"Bekah!" Dolores called. "C'mon, hon. You're gonna make me late!"

The voice startled Bekah. Heart pounding, she jammed the bills into her pocket and ran to her own room. She hid the cash in a baggie with a lighter and pipe in a thermos, screwed the lid on tight. She would stash it in her locker at school.

"Bekah!"

"I'm coming!" She sailed past Dolores at the bottom of the stairs, who followed her as she ran out to the car.

"I've got all my memory verses memorized." Darcy smiled at Dolores in the front seat as they drove to the high school.

"That's my girl!" Dolores turned to the back seat. "Did you hear that, Bekah? Are you ready with your memory verses for tonight?"

"That's my little golden girl!" Bekah mimicked.

"Hey, why are you being so mean?" Darcy said.

*What a freaking suck-up. What a waste of time.* "No, I'm not ready," Bekah said in a voice filled with scorn.

"No?" Dolores took her eyes from the road to study her daughter. "Why not? What have you been doing with your time since last week's Awana?"

*Not memorizing stupid scripture,* she thought. *I hate Awana. I hate the kids who go to Awana.* "You never asked me if I wanted to belong." She glared at Dolores. "I'm not going anymore. I quit."

"You *quit?*" Darcy twisted to see her sister in the back seat. "Can we quit?" she asked Dolores.

"No, you cannot. That is not an option. Your father is the minister of the church. You are certainly not allowed to quit."

"Not allowed?" Bekah laughed without mirth.

"We'll just see about that, young lady," Dolores replied, pulling into the school drop-off lane.

Bekah said nothing, but sat sullen in the back seat.

In front of the high school, Dolores stopped her car in a line of vehicles. Darcy kissed her mother and ran to catch up to friends walking toward the building.

As Bekah slammed the door behind her, Dolores pushed a button to roll down the window.

"No goodbye?" she said with a smile that was clearly artificial to Bekah.

"No happy birthday?" Bekah shot back.

Dolores's sunny façade slipped.

"Yeah, of course you wouldn't be on top of the whole birthday thing. You weren't there."

Dolores sniffed, held her chin high. "Don't forget, I'll be here at three o'clock to pick you up."

Bekah bent to look into the car at the woman she called her mother, the woman who had adopted her years ago and took her mother's place. Her voice was icy. "You can come, Dolores, but I won't be here."

Dolores wore her shock pitifully. "Oh! My Lord! Your father will be very angry." Then, as if the most hurtful part of Bekah's rebellion had just registered, her eyes filled with tears and she said in a high-pitched voice, "Since when have you started calling me Dolores?"

"Since I turned 18. Happy birthday to me," Bekah said. "It didn't seem to bother you when I started calling my own mother *Jane*."

Dolores blinked through her tears. "How many times have I reminded you over the years, that Jane threw you and Darcy away?" She wiped at first one eye, then the other. Face now full of earnestness, she said, "Honey, you know what your dad said. You brought this curfew on yourself for sneaking out and going to that basketball game. You know he said you couldn't go—but you went anyway. Again and again, you flaunt our rules. It just can't go on."

"I really don't give a flying rat's ass about your rules anymore."

Dolores' jaw dropped and she drew in her breath. "Bekah! Language . . ."

She rolled her eyes. "Puh-lease. He told me I couldn't go to the game—because I hadn't cleaned my room. Then when I went anyway, he *came to the gym and got me in front of all my friends*, saying I needed to come home and make my bed and clean my room."

Dolores pleaded, "You knew you needed to do that before you left for the game."

"He had to come to the school and get me?"

"You know the rules."

"Yeah, whatever. Over the past few months, I've been thinking about lots of bad times in my life, including that day. When we got home, you were standing there with him. Remember?"

Dolores said nothing, her mouth a tight line.

"You agreed he had the right to come and get me in the middle of the game. Embarrass me in front of all my friends. That's messed up." She glared at Dolores. "You know it was all because you both didn't want me socializing with heathens. He was being a dick—and you stood by him."

Dolores' head jerked back as if she'd seen a dead animal. "You watch your mouth, young lady!"

Bekah scowled, shook her head as if to say *if swearing is your big concern, you are underestimating the reality of our situation.*

"Bekah, you used to be happy. And you'd *never* talked that way. What's got into you lately?"

Bekah did not answer. She shifted her backpack and trudged to the high school building.

A war was being waged inside of Bekah Churlick and she felt little of the battle raging within. For many weeks, her subconscious had fought fiercely with her conscious mind for the upper hand in daily combat. In the last few weeks, against all odds, her subconscious had won.

When the yoke of life-long programming was thrown off, she felt a sweet sense of freedom. Her new emotional independence cut loose the restraints that had molded her behavior, her language, and made it possible for her to live peacefully with Logan and Dolores Churlick for six years.

At noon, Bekah sat with a few friends at a long lunchroom table. Chatter and laughter several decibels above the classroom filled the air. Administrators stood at their posts around the cafeteria.

Izzy, a friend who was in Spanish class with Bekah, grabbed for her thermos on the table.

Sketcher, Bekah's bosom buddy since kindergarten, punched her on the arm.

"Ouch!" Izzy said, rubbing her bicep. "That's my pitching arm, you shithead!"

Sketcher snatched the thermos from the middle of the table where Bekah had placed it as notification that they would be getting high after lunch. They would skip a period or two, or possibly the rest of the afternoon as they smoked pot down by the river. "Then don't be so grabby with Bekah's stash."

"Good God, Sketcher," Bekah said, "you want to get us busted? Try lowering your voice."

"They can't hear us," Sketcher said. "Listen to how loud it is. Like, they just want to make sure another food fight doesn't break out."

He pushed the remainder of his sandwich into his mouth and washed it down with a small carton of chocolate milk. "Hey, there's an assembly on Friday before the game. Who can score some weed?"

"I've got some stuff in my car," Izzy said.

"Sweet." Bekah held out her hand for the thermos. Sketcher placed it in her palm and she slid it into her backpack. "See you at the place in about 15 minutes."

That evening, Reverend Logan Churlick received a call from the attendance office saying that Bekah had not attended any of her classes that afternoon.

"In fact, recent records show there is a pattern of her missing the period after lunch. Doctor's appointments? But besides that, it seems recently she's missed most or all of her afternoon classes." The woman paused. "She is a senior and may have senioritis—but still. Maybe there's something else going on?"

Logan looked up from the phone on the kitchen wall not far from where Dolores was, her back to him, yellow rubber gloved hands immersed in soapy water. She turned off the water and faced him, concern etched in her brow. Darcy stood next to her, a towel hanging from her hand.

He frowned and said slowly, "That doesn't sound like our Bekah." The expression that took over Dolores' face told him that it sounded exactly like their Bekah. He sighed. "We'll get to the bottom of this. Appreciate the call."

He hung up and asked, "Darcy, do you know where your sister is?"

She looked up at her father from under dark lashes and hesitated. Logan read this as a moment in which she weighed her loyalty to her sister versus her duty to her parents—and to God. His frown deepened.

"No," she said. "She has her friends, I have mine."

Dolores tried to resurrect the contentious discussion of earlier in the day, but Logan stopped her with a wave of his hand. "We've already discussed her rebellious attitude and how she refused to meet you after school, Dolores. We'll see what she has to say for herself. I don't have a good feeling about this." His hard eyes spoke of the punishment already planned.

Darcy said in a meek voice, "I hope she's okay. Can we pray?"

Reverend Churlick and his wife stared at their daughter, their faces registering shock at Darcy's concern about Bekah's well-being and her desire to bring the situation back from punitive to pious. Her words seemed to shame them.

Logan recovered in an instant and, in a magnanimous gesture, held out his hands. Dolores and Darcy stepped into his embrace and bowed their heads in the tiny kitchen.

A short time later, Bekah walked in the front door stoned, eyes still dilated, and her parents were waiting for her.

2

Bekah finished dialing the numbers and butterflies barrel rolled through her stomach. Something caught her eye. She glanced up from where she sat on her parents' bed and hung up in disgust.

"You know the therapist said you have to give me privacy." She glared at Dolores, who was standing in the doorway.

"But sugar plum, I was just putting these towels . . ."

Bekah stood and pointed toward the door. "I'm getting my mom back. And there's nothing you or Dad can do about it—besides ordering me to make the call from this phone so you can listen on the other line." Anger rose in her. She felt keenly her position of helplessness, even when she had finally achieved a position of strength.

Dolores stood frozen in the doorway, blinking back tears.

"Leave!" Without ceremony, Bekah walked over, shut the door, and went back to the phone.

Bekah had admitted on the evening of her birthday that she smoked pot. "What kind of Christian daughter acts this way?" her father had shouted, exhorting that she needed fixing: her disrespectful attitude, her swearing, breaking their rules, poor grades. And now drugs.

Bekah responded that his self-righteous piousness made her want to puke.

Dolores and Logan Churlick were so rattled they agreed to send her to a secular therapist. They'd felt they had no choice when she had spat, "I'm not going to any *Christian* shrink."

At the therapist's office, Bekah had sat up straight and strong, her auburn hair brushing her squared shoulders.

"I want to talk to my *real* mom," she said. "I don't really care how much I piss off Dad and Dolores."

"I'm confused," Dr. Likely said. "Is Reverend Churlick your real dad?"

"Yes."

"Then Mrs. Churlick is your stepmother?"

"No. When my mom gave us up, Dolores adopted us legally."

Dr. Likely sat back in his chair and raised his eyebrows. "I see."

"My sister and I turned into these hateful little brats. When Jane—"

"Who's Jane?"

Bekah looked away, embarrassed. She thought for a moment about how to explain how she and Darcy came to call their mother Jane. "We lived with our mom and we'd always called her Mom. But long before the end, we started calling her Jane, telling her she was only our biological mother. We called Dolores our true Christian mother. When Jane would try to reason with us, we'd just spout scripture back at her. Every day it was war. We'd do the shittiest things we could think of to make her cry or get mad or . . ." Bekah took a deep breath, bowed her head.

"When we were 12, my mom and dad got into a custody battle. Since Darcy and I were Bible-thumping fundamentalist Christians, we wanted Dad to win and wanted nothing to do with Jane. We believed she was under the influence of Satan and demons."

Dr. Likely frowned. "How do you mean 'under the influence'?"

Bekah fidgeted in her seat. "I don't know, exactly. I just knew that since she didn't go to our church, she wasn't a Christian and that meant she would go to the fiery pit of hell and damnation. I mean, it was so real to me, I could hear the screeching demons. Besides all that, she was a baby killer."

"A baby killer? Did she have an abortion?"

"No, no. She was pro-choice. We were taught that meant she was a baby killer."

"I see. Go on."

"We heard nasty put downs about her every day, many times a day, from Dad and Dolores. But, of course, we never mentioned that to the GAL who worked for the court on our case.

"I remember this: my mom was my very best friend, I mean I really loved my mom—and somehow we came to hate her. Darcy and I were deathly afraid of going to hell if we kept living with her. So we did everything we could to make her life hell—for almost a year, until she gave us up to Dad."

Dr. Likely wore a serious expression, seeming to weigh every word Bekah said. Such circumstances were rare, and he was getting an inside look, limited though it was, at how such a family catastrophe had happened.

"Now, it's like the fear that dominated me, the hatred of Jane, has broken apart inside. I've been thinking of her a lot lately and really want to reconnect."

"So what's keeping you from doing that?"

Bekah examined the man with the bushy brows sitting in the chair facing her and wondered if she could speak the truth. Then, impulsively, she decided, *What have I got to lose?*

"For years, we thought our mother didn't love us. She couldn't, or she would never have given us up. And as long as we've lived with Dad, we were forbidden from contacting Jane.

Dr. Likely sat back in his chair, face wreathed in disbelief. "Forbidden? Why?"

"Well, she's a heathen. My dad's a minister. We were told that she would lead us off the path of righteousness and take us with her straight to hell."

Dr. Likely said nothing.

"Six years without her, I mean, I don't feel like I really know her anymore. Don't know if she'd even want me. But lately, something in me is just screaming to connect with my real mom."

The vague memory of Jane had, in recent months, been playing over and over in Bekah's mind, and strangely, it filled her with a shimmering mirage of hope—and with fear. The thought of her mother rejecting her, because she knew full well she deserved it, filled her with agony. Still, the hope of reconnecting would not let go; it felt safe and good and right.

Bekah faced the therapist, his fingertips steepled, his look thoughtful, sympathetic. She was dying to know if this time dealing with an adult would be different. Which way would this therapy session go? Would he see her parents as protective and loving? Would he agree with them that her past was causing her rebelliousness and she should leave it alone so that her life could settle back into its peaceful somnambulistic routine?

He said, "I don't know why you shouldn't talk to your mom. Is there any reason that contacting her seems unsafe for you to do so?"

Bekah couldn't speak. She shook her head, then said, "Oh no, not at all. She was never unsafe, just unsaved."

Logan and Dolores Churlick were taken aback when the therapist, instead of waving a magic wand to fix the incorrigible Bekah, firmly suggested she be allowed to phone her mother that very evening.

Bekah sat on the edge of her parents' bed and dialed her mother's number. She held her breath and her heartbeat quickened. *I wonder if I'll be able to talk? What if she rejects me?* She let out a shaky breath. *What if she hates me for everything I said and did so long ago?*

Across the state of Washington, the phone rang. Bolivar was in the kitchen working on dinner. Jane called out, "I'll get it," and sprawled full length across the bed to pick up the receiver.

"Hello?"

The line was silent a moment, then the sound Jane heard took her breath away.

"Hello, Mom? It's Bekah."

Shock washed through Jane. She pressed the receiver tightly to her ear, not trusting she had heard correctly, the words ricocheting in her mind.

Bekah's voice, the last time they had been together, had the reedy sound of a twelve-year-old, not the voice she heard now. This was an adult voice coming through the phone. This young woman was her Bekah. Her little girl was a young woman now. *My God*, she realized, wiping at the tears running down her cheeks, *she called me Mom! Not Jane. Mom.*

Jane tried to speak, cleared her dry throat and tried again.

"Bekah?" she said, voice thick with emotion.

"It's me."

"Oh, Bekah!" The moment was like some surrealistic Dali painting of two women, their hearts outside their bodies, spindly arms straining toward each other, connected by a telephone line resembling an umbilical cord across a fantastic dreamscape. "Oh, honey, I can't believe it's *you!*"

"Oh, Mom!" Bekah's words tumbled out of her, colored with relief and bliss. "You don't know what a comfort it is to hear joy in your voice rather than the anger I deserve. Just hearing your voice, I mean, I can't tell you how great it is just to hear you. It makes me want to cry, hearing the voice I know so well."

"So—is everything all right, sweetheart?"

"Everything's all right now. Dad and Dolores decided they couldn't handle me anymore, so they sent me to a shrink. Today was my first session, and I told my therapist I wanted to talk to you. That's why I was finally allowed to call you."

The statement sent a jolt of anger through Jane. Bekah was saying she hadn't been allowed to call until an advocate had stepped in. But Jane gave the anger a quick kick aside to return to the miracle of the moment. She was talking to her estranged daughter, who for six years had hated her. Somehow, Bekah had managed to hold onto the memory of her mother's love. Nothing was going to spoil this moment, not even righteous anger.

Jane bubbled with questions about school and friends and Bekah's life. And her daughter answered all of them. As Jane listened, she felt a bright, radiating joy thrumming through her.

When Bo came in and put his hand on her shoulder, she said "Bekah!" and put her hand on his.

After 30 minutes of chatting and laughing, Bekah said, "Hold on, Mom." Jane could hear a muffled voice in a background: "I've paid enough for this long-distance call. You need to hang up."

In a tight voice, Bekah relayed her father's edict to Jane, who said, "No problem, hon. Let's hang up and I'll call you right back."

Bekah hung up the phone and said in a withering voice, "I'll let my therapist know about your generosity. My mom is calling right back, so you can leave."

Humiliation and anger fought for control on Logan's face.

"Disappointed we haven't even mentioned you? Go on back to where you and Dolores are listening in on the other line so you don't miss anything."

The phone rang and she said to her father, "The cat is *so* out of the bag."

They talked for three more hours. Bekah told Jane all about her teachers, the kids she hung out with and what they did for fun, that her favorite food was still her mother's bullfrog ta-cos (pronounced with a long A), and that she had won several awards for her artwork.

Finally, Jane asked, "What about Darcy? Is she—"

Bekah sighed. "Sorry, Mom. Maybe with time..." But the way she let the words trail off, made Jane's heart fall to its knees.

Before they hung up, they made plans for Bekah to come see her in western Washington. She would come to visit Jane for a ski trip over spring break. Both were wild with anticipation at seeing each other for a week, beginning the following weekend.

Bolivar was taking tacos from the microwave when Jane walked into the kitchen. "Hope you don't mind, but I couldn't wait."

"Huh? No, I don't mind. I'm in a fog," she said, hugging herself. "A deliriously happy fog."

"You do seem to be sort of floating."

She sat down at the table and absently stirred the guacamole until it turned green again.

Bolivar brought the reheated tacos over, poured her a drink, and uncovered the cheese and slaw. "What?" he asked, noticing her frown.

Jane looked up at him. "Bekah's the only one I talked with. Darcy is still—she's still brainwashed."

Bolivar squeezed her shoulder. He had witnessed Jane change over the years from the woman she had once been. She was not as giving, quicker to find fault, to judge. The loss of her girls broke her heart in such a way that when time eventually put the jagged pieces back together, she was marked.

Bo, whose own heart beat to the rhythm of Jane's words, her tears, her broken spirit, was also broken by the loss. As hard as it was for Bo to accept the changes in Jane, his love gave him no choice. Now, they would celebrate Bekah's return, and continue to grieve the loss of Darcy. They would get through the years ahead, and no matter what life had in store, he was certain they would create new meaning, for theirs was an eternal love.

# 3

The following Saturday, Jane pulled up at the McDonalds in Ellensburg, the halfway point between Rathcreek in eastern Washington and Berry Valley, a small town in western Washington. Logan's Peugeot was parked in the lot. The door flew open and long, skinny legs unfolded from the interior. Bekah stood, and Jane took her in: the long, auburn hair, her slender build, and a million watt smile. She hurried to her daughter.

"Oh my God, Bekah! *Look* at you!" Jane said, wrapping her arms around her.

"Mom!" Bekah's voice was muffled in the folds of Jane's jacket. She held Jane tightly.

They retrieved her suitcase from the trunk of her father's car. In her excited state, Bekah did not even say good-bye to her father, did not even look back as she climbed into Jane's car. After the three-hour drive Logan had made to bring her to her mother, it was as if he didn't exist. Jane did not trust herself to speak to Logan, and so did not.

On the drive home, Bekah said, "Why did you move to the western side of the state? You and Bo lived in Rathcreek or Spokane your whole lives."

Jane took her eyes off the road a moment. "I couldn't stay," she said simply. "I had to get away after . . ."

Bekah saw the pain.

"The move gave us a fresh start, far from Rathcreek. We like it here. It's like entering the real world after living in a cave your whole life." Jane laughed.

Bekah nodded. "That pretty much describes Rathcreek."

"So first, Bo got hired to teach in Olympia, then I got hired by Berry Valley High School. My students, they-a call-a me *Mama Bernardo*," Jane said in an Italian accent, holding her thumb to her fingers. "What?" Her smile faded as she noticed Bekah's worried look.

"Oh nothing," said Bekah. "I'm just being a baby. I feel like now that I have you back in my life, I'm kind of jealous of your students who might've wormed their way into your heart." With a guilty smile she said, "I want you all to myself."

"Oh, trust me. You have me, my darling daughter."

Bekah studied her mom's profile. There were fine lines at the outside corner of her eye. She was older—how could she not be? But essentially, she looked the same: shoulder-length chestnut hair shining in a neon halo of copper highlights from the light coming through the sun roof. The turned-up corners of her mouth made her look like she was holding in a joke.

"What's that?" Jane asked, pointing to Bekah's ankle.

"This?" she touched an ankle bracelet woven of colorful threads. "It's a chastity reminder. I took a vow of chastity and that's to remind me."

Jane smiled and shook her head a little as though she didn't understand. "Really? A reminder? On your ankle?"

She was silent a moment, then said with a little smile, "So, does it work?"

Bekah's head snapped up. "I'm a virgin!"

"Whoa, honey, I'm just trying to get to know you." She trained her eyes back on the freeway. "But I am glad you're not sexually active. I have a junior and a sophomore who are pregnant. By the looks of it, they may not graduate. Starting life out as a single mom is rough."

Bekah said quietly, "Life as a mom was a lot harder for you than it should've been." Voice faltering, she added, "I'm so sorry, Mom."

Jane's heart fluttered, as it did every time Bekah called her *Mom*. She marveled at the miracle of having her daughter seated next to her.

She patted her daughter's arm and was silent, afraid that if she tried to speak, she would cry. Finally, she said in a thick voice, "Thanks, Bekah. That means a lot to me. I can't even tell you what it feels like to have you in my life again. It's like you gave me back my heart and I can feel it beating."

Bekah wiped her eyes and squeezed her mother's hand.

They drove in silence a while, each woman existing in her dark privacy. "That wasn't really you," Jane said. "You weren't yourself. You were—"

"A perfect little shit."

Jane was jolted by the swear word, then she gave her daughter a little smile. "True." She signaled to move into the far left lane. "Bekah—"

"Yeah?"

"How did it happen? Can you remember?" She had an insatiable need to know the story behind her daughters' alienation. At the same time, she wanted to spare Bekah the pain such a conversation would bring up. "Wait. I don't want to start off our time together talking about that."

Bekah closed her eyes, scratched an eyebrow. Finally, she said, "How was I so totally under the spell that I believed you weren't the mother I knew and loved? I don't know, except I think that questioning whether or not you were a real Christian started the unraveling. Not to mention all the constant bad mouthing we heard about you. I mean I had a real fear of hell. It felt like Dad was our only protection from you taking Darcy and me with you to burn forever. You know, the screeching demons and eternal fire and brimstone were very real to me. But why did it replace all the truth? Why was I so blind to everything good we knew about you? I don't know how that happened, I really don't. What I do know now is that it was all a crock of shit."

Jane's lips tightened and she looked to the horizon ahead where purple and gold mountains stood outlined by the sunset in the west.

"Hey, cracker butt!" Bo said, giving Bekah a bear hug. "Welcome home."

The look on Bekah's face said that the nickname took her by surprise. She laughed. "How's the boxcar butt doin'?"

Bo laughed. "Fine. Just fine—now that you're here." He brought her suitcase into the house.

Jane hugged Bo and gave him a kiss.

"Mmm-mmm," Bekah said, sniffing.

"I went domestic during your absence," he said to Jane. "Baked some chocolate chip cookies. Hope they're edible."

"You are a spoiler," Jane said. "Milk?" she asked them.

"Milk," said Bekah.

"Me, too," said Bolivar.

They sat around the kitchen table eating and reminiscing about the good days, when Bekah was a little girl.

"Just pinch me," Jane said. "Better yet—Bo, take a picture of Bekah and me." She gave her cell phone to Bolivar, scooted her chair next to Bekah's, and put her arm around her shoulders.

Bekah was rigid and frowning.

"What's the matter, honey? Don't tell me you've grown camera shy."

Bekah squirmed out from under Jane's arm. "I can't," she said. "It just feels weird."

"What do you mean?" Bo asked, peering up from the phone's camera.

She faced them, chin trembling. "With my mouth shut, my smile looks fake. With teeth showing, it's worse."

Jane felt a surge of protective anger for her daughter. She glanced at Bo.

"I'm used to being criticized in a thousand ways," Bekah said. "It was drilled into me that as far as photos went, I was a failure. My smile, my squinting eyes. In fact . . . nothing about me was ever good enough."

"Oh ho! *That's* why you were sent to a therapist," Bo said. "Imperfection is a real bitch."

Bekah grinned at Bo.

Jane held out her arm and said, "Just smile, honey. Any way you do it, you're beautiful."

At first, Bekah did not move, as if not trusting her new reality. She brushed cookie crumbs from the table in front of her. Slowly, she dragged her chair next to her mother's. And when Bo brought the camera back up, she smiled.

Bekah reached for another cookie. "So the reason I was sent to the therapist is that I'm a real pain in the ass to them. I don't even try to be good anymore."

Jane was silent, her mind open to wherever Bekah's story might take them.

"It's been a while now since I realized all the 'going to hell' stuff just stopped making me scared. Since everything I did was bad, I figured, what did I have to lose? Why not be *really* bad? Smoke pot. Skip class." She looked from Jane to Bo, as if waiting for a reaction.

"Smoke pot?" Bo asked. Jane elbowed him and nodded for Bekah to go on.

"About six months ago, I got my license and asked if I could drive over to see you. I didn't know you lived six hours away. But, still. Know what they told me?"

"What?" Jane asked.

"They said they didn't think I was strong enough."

"Jesus Christ." Bo shook his head.

Jane had told herself that since she had Bekah back in her life, she would not wage war with Logan, putting their daughter in the middle. There had been no contact with him for six years. She would not start now.

With effort, she pushed down her anger and shifted her attention to this moment. "Well," she said, "I guess his pipeline to God must be broken. You look pretty strong to me."

# 4

On the spring day Bekah and Jane planned to go snow skiing, the morning was raucous with the drone of the tiller engine as Bolivar made his way through the garden. Bundled up in their ski gear, she and Bekah loaded the car. Jane kissed Bo good-bye and he gave Bekah a side-armed hug.

"You two have fun," he said.

"Are you sure you don't want to come?" Jane asked.

"Nah. I've got to get the ground in shape for planting those starts before they get so big they jump out of their little peat pots and plant themselves."

Jane knew the ground was just barely thawed from the brutal winter they'd endured. He had begun his tilling much earlier than usual—to allow her and Bekah time alone.

On the slopes of Crystal Mountain, Jane remembered how much she loved skiing. She had packed away her skis when her girls were no longer part of her life. The memory of teaching her little five-year-olds to ski down a hill as she guided them between her legs was too much.

Jane and Bekah rode the chair lift. "God, I've missed you, Bekah. It's like I'm in a dream. I can feel that kind of dream-like super excitement bubbling up whenever I look at you. The only thing missing is that we can't fly." She gave her daughter a wry smile. "When's the last time you went skiing?"

Bekah blinked and said, "With you."

"Really? I didn't think your dad and Dolores skied, but all that snow over there and no ski trips with your friends?"

"Oh, Mom," Bekah said, shaking her head. "You don't understand." She swung her legs and her long skis scissored the air as the chair lift pulled them up the mountainside.

"When I went to live with Dad, everything else fell away. All that I had, all that I was, was focused on God." She turned her goggled face to her mother. "I didn't have ski buddies anymore. All my ski buddies were secular. You know what that meant, right?"

Jane nodded, beginning to grasp how much her daughter's life had changed.

They rode the chairlift up the mountain in silence. The trees on the hillside were so white, it hurt their eyes. Thick, snowy branches dared the sun to prove the cusp of another season was upon them. It would not be long before the trees marching up the snowy mountain would belong to the future of warm days and green grass.

Jane said, "Do you remember when you told me, 'I'm a Christian now?' And I asked, what happened to honoring your father *and* mother?"

"And I told you that you took that passage out of context," Bekah said. "The Bible says parents should not bring their children to wrath."

Jane recalled that her young daughter had looked at her with malice, eyes glazed, voice flat and emotionless. For the first time, she knew her Bekah was not there. "For me, it was heartbreaking, but for you—"

"It was victory in the *Lord!*" Bekah said, jabbing her ski pole toward the clear blue sky.

"No matter how much I pleaded or reasoned, cried or scolded, nothing could pierce the godly armor you and your sister had wrapped yourselves in."

Bekah giggled. "What a little shit I was."

Jane said softly, "I could've handled a little shit of a teenage daughter. But our bond was gone. It was like I was dealing with a zombie."

She shook her head. "The final straw was when your sister wrote a letter to *her real parents* in Rathcreek and I intercepted it. The letter said: 'I hate Jane! If I don't get out of here soon, I'm going to kill her or myself. Get me OUT of here!' That's when I started locking my bedroom door at night."

"Oh my God. That's awful, Mom." Bekah was silent a moment, then turned to her mother. "You know, I never really questioned this before, but they sort of kept anything from getting through to us to undo the hatred and fear of you. Now I get it. That's why Darcy and I were forbidden from checking for messages on the answering machine or checking for mail in the mailbox."

Jane felt a jolt in her chest. "Are you kidding me? You couldn't check the mailbox or answering machine for six years?"

Bekah nodded. "That's right. He said you'd contact us and manipulate us."

Jane shook her head, filled with anger and the irony of the situation. *Manipulate?* She tried to grasp the full extent

Logan and Dolores had gone to, to make sure she never had a chance to influence her own children to love her.

She nudged Bekah, signaling that they would soon be disembarking from the chairlift. She scooted to the edge of the chair, her mittened hand on the armrest, ready to push off. They sailed smoothly down the incline and readied themselves to tackle the slope.

Maneuvering in skis had come back to them both, as though they'd come to the mountains together yesterday rather than so long ago. The old habits they shared, like comfortable old lives they now inhabited again, slipped on easily.

"No more reminiscing about the dark ages," Jane said. "We're going forward. I don't want to ruin a good day on the slopes, especially if it's been six years since you've had skis on your feet!"

Bekah said, "Beat you down!" and took off down the slope.

Jane planted her poles and chased her down the hill. The moguls slowed her some, but she managed not to fall. It was hard to concentrate on the snowy hillside. The conversation she and Bekah had started insisted on playing in her head to its finish.

The more Jane talked with Bekah, the more the grief and guilt she had lived with began to crumble. She could finally let go of the image of the shocked court-appointed Guardian Ad Litem, questioning her judgment about giving up her parental rights so the girls could go live with their father. She saw, if the GAL couldn't, that her daughters were being torn apart. To the GAL, the Churlicks were blameless. But she knew Logan and Dolores would continue to poison the girls. Apparently, removing herself as their target had worked. Her Bekah was back. With any luck, before long, Darcy would be, too.

She hurtled herself down the mountainside after Bekah. She breathed deeply, thankful for not only her daughter, but for Bolivar, who had helped preserve enough of herself to have something left to give to Bekah.

# 5

Bekah sat on the kitchen counter while Jane prepared dinner, keeping her company as she had done as a little girl. Billy Joel played on Pandora, as he usually did while Jane fixed dinner.

"I can't get over what a good skier you are!" Jane said, chopping garlic.

"It was just so fun! I didn't know if I'd remember how to ski after so much time, but it came right back. What are you making?"

"A kale casserole. You haven't had it before, but I think you'll like it. It's got onions, garlic, Yukon gold potatoes, and sun dried tomatoes. All sautéed with the kale, of course. It'll be killah with the salmon Bo's going to barbeque."

"Sounds, ah, interesting." Bekah was quiet a moment, then said, "I doubt I'm going to like it. You *know* how I feel about vegetables."

Jane looked up from her chopping. It suddenly came back to her that the twins hated most vegetables when they were little. Peas and corn were about all she could get them to eat. "Well, your taste buds might have changed. You can try a bite, can't you?"

Bekah nodded, her look doubtful. She watched her mom scrape the chopped onion and garlic into a sauté pan. The pieces sizzled and the aroma filled the kitchen.

"I don't want this week to end, Mom."

Jane stopped her stirring and turned the heat down. Her heartbeat seemed a little louder, thudding in her chest. "I know. Neither do I."

"No, I mean I don't want to go back."

"What?"

"I-I can't go back. I hate it there."

"Bekah, you've only got a couple months before you graduate. You can't just—"

"You don't understand, Mom." Bekah looked pitiful, sitting on the counter like a little girl, eyes welling with tears. "For me, during those years apart, it was like I lost a huge chunk of my childhood. There's a hole where the mother-daughter talks we should have had about getting my first bra and starting my period should be. Now I have you back in my life, and I just want to hold on."

"Tell me about it," Jane said. "During those empty years, whenever I saw mothers and daughters together in the mall, I felt like crying. That should've been *us*, laughing and talking as we shopped for the perfect pair of shoes for the school dance. You don't know how many times I wished I could have you back."

Bekah said, "My life changed so much. I thought we were going to church a lot when we'd go over to visit Dad for a weekend. But when we lived there, we'd go to church around five times a week. More, if there was any special stuff like revivals. And forget about getting to choose my own friends."

Bekah looked out the window at two hummingbirds at the feeder. The birds buzzed around it, one chasing the other, until they zipped off together into the bright blue sky.

Jane studied her daughter, sitting in the cheery yellow kitchen. *She looks the way she did when she was a little girl. I wish I could see the sadness and loss inside her. But she seems so strong. Scares me a little, but it's her fiery spirit that broke her free so she could come back to me.*

Bekah was quiet, her look inward. She seemed to be fighting emotions coming back to life inside her. "One time, Dad told me, 'Bekah, you might as well face it, you're anorexic.' After that, he said I had to drink five glasses of whole milk every day. Every—*fucking*—day! Now, I'm allergic to milk."

"Oh God, Bekah!" Jane said, shocked both about Logan's punitive order as well as her daughter's foul mouth. Since when did Bekah use the "f" word? She wanted to chastise her. But fear gripped her. *She's an adult now. Do I really want to take on this issue?*

Jane felt paralyzed, unsure of the mothering instinct that had come so naturally to her in the past. She wanted more than anything to provide a peaceful atmosphere that would draw her daughter closer as they got to know each other, not a critical one that might push her away. Back to her chopping, she said simply, "But you're built slender like me."

"*Du-uh!* I think he wanted to rub out any trace of you in me."

Bekah took a slice of red bell pepper from the pile on the cutting board, munched it, and making a face, threw it into the sink. "And forget about shopping for shoes in the mall. I wasn't allowed to go to high school dances. We were discouraged from having secular friends, see? And we'd get grilled about what church our friends went to. Then Dad and Dolores would do research to see if that branch of Christianity lined up with ours." She hung her head and murmured, "They worked on me and worked on me, until I finally told Beth, my best friend, that I didn't think we should hang out together anymore."

Jane's heart sickened. She stopped chopping and looked at Bekah.

Bekah sighed and went on. "But through it all, stuck in my mind's underground, were our last moments together, in the church that day. Remember? You read us the parting letter you gave us. Of course, it was trashed as soon as we left the church. Anyway, you said when I was 16 and got my driver's license, I-I could—" she swallowed, "drive over to visit you."

Jane put the chef's knife down and placed her arms around Bekah. She stroked her hair, tears in both of their eyes.

When the week ended, Bekah called her father, saying she refused to go back to Rathcreek, insisting she wasn't wanted anyway and she could finish up the last couple of months of high school in Berry Valley.

Logan was silent on the other end of the line, then in a deliberate voice said, "Let me speak to the woman you call your *mother.*"

Bekah handed the phone to Jane, who sat on a kitchen chair nearby, elbows on knees, palms cupping her chin. She was nervous, but she sat up straight. She was prepared to be the support Bekah needed.

"You think since Bekah calls you her *mother* now that I'm going to sit still while you steal her away from me?" Logan began, then his voice softened. "I'm her father, Jane. You know how much my girls mean to me. How can you take her from me when I've only got a couple more months before she leaves the nest?"

Jane hesitated. She knew Logan loved his daughter. The sound of sorrow in his voice moved her. "I've tried to talk to her, but her mind's made up. It's only a couple months. And it's really her decision, anyway, don't you think?"

"The court says she's mine until she graduates," he said. "You give her back to me, or I'll take you to court."

*Here's the Logan I know*, she thought. "I guess you have to do what you have to do."

"Did you hear me? I'll have you thrown in jail!" he shouted.

She could imagine the color rising in his face, the veins standing out on his neck. "Go for it. After throwing lots of money at your lawyer defending your right to drag Bekah back to Rathcreek, the judge will say that at 18, she's emancipated and can choose to live here with us."

He was silent a moment, then said, "I'll make you regret this, Jane. You steal my daughter away, I won't pay for her college education."

But she would not be blackmailed. "Face it, Logan, your magic God failed."

"Well, you may win this round, but you'll *never* get Darcy!" he said in an ominous voice that froze Jane's blood. She could hear Dolores in the background shrilling, "Never! Not ever!"

Later, when Jane shared her worry about Darcy with Bolivar, he chuckled self-confidently and said, "What, like if you hand over Bekah, he's going to put in a good word with Darcy for you?"

She smiled weakly.

"He has no idea what Darcy's future holds. Neither do we," he said. "But I know this: if Bekah can come around, Darcy can."

Jane sighed with contentment. Bolivar could do that for her, take a bad situation, make her laugh about it, and give her the big picture, a much less worrisome perspective than her own.

When Jane told Bekah her father would not pay toward her college education, her daughter laughed, saying, "It's not like I've applied to any. He knows that. I'm not exactly a four point like Darcy and Simon. I've never planned to go to college. I'm going to find a job. But I'll tell you this: he took my mother from me—for years. If he thinks I still want to be a loving daughter to him, he's dead wrong."

Bekah transferred her records to the local high school and graduated in June. In the summer, she found a job at Zumiez, a skateboard shop in the Tacoma Mall.

She settled into life with Jane and Bo. However, being a rebel was a persona she found hard to give up. Though the eye rolling grew less automatic and her confidence was strengthening, the pendulum of Bekah's rebellious response to her Rathcreek upbringing swung not as quickly back to contentment as Jane and Bo might have liked.

Jane knew Bekah was regularly partaking of marijuana and hanging out with new friends that Jane knew from her classroom at the high school. Jane did not consider the friends to be good role models and, while efforts were underway to legalize marijuana in the state, smoking pot was currently illegal. But she felt there was not much she could do without alienating her daughter. So she simply stewed in her anxiety, hoping a time would come that she and Bekah could have a serious conversation about her use of an illegal substance.

Bolivar was not so understanding. "Jane, you've got to do something about this pot smoking." He sat facing her on the red couch that dominated the living room where she was reading the latest *New Yorker*.

She put down her magazine and took off her glasses. "What can I do? It's not like I can control my adult daughter. Besides, lots of kids smoke pot—we're pretty lucky she's being open about it and not hiding it from us."

Aware Bekah was out with friends that evening, he raised his voice. "I don't care if she is an adult and if every eighteen-year-old we know is smoking it. But I do care if your daughter, who lives with us, is a pot-head. I don't want her to influence Simon when he comes home from the university on break."

A fire ignited in Jane's belly. "So you're only interested in this because of how it affects your precious Simon?"

Bo reached out to her. "That's not the only reason. I'm sorry—I shouldn't have said it that way."

She snatched her shoulder away. "Who are you calling a pot-head?"

"Bekah." He ran his hand through his hair. "Have you thought about this, Jane? Who knows what else she's doing, out till two in the morning?"

Jane snapped, "Is it a crime for her to stay out late when she doesn't have to get up early—because she's looking for work?"

"What if she's drinking? At 18, that's against the law, too. As long as she lives under my roof, I can't condone her breaking the law. What if she's riding with friends who've been drinking? Do you know anything about the crowd she hangs out with? How many boys has she been with?"

"How many *boys?*" Jane shrilled. "What are you saying? That my daughter's promiscuous?" The fire was consuming her. Any possibility of her remaining calm, drawing logical conclusions in the face of Bo's remarks, had turned into a smoldering pile of rubble inside her.

"I'm just saying she's out getting high all the time, and that makes girls vulnerable. As a teacher, you know that. I know it, too. I've had talks with my students about this kind of behavior."

In the past, she would have known her husband was right. If Bekah weren't her daughter, if she were her student, Jane would have been able to see the red flags. But fear had her in its monstrous grip and it was impossible for her to say something that could cause Bekah to turn from her.

"You are such a hypocrite!"

Bo flinched, but his expression said he'd had enough of her.

She said, "You smoked pot when you were young. I've smoked pot—"

"You've smoked pot exactly once."

"So? We've both tried it. Why can't Bekah? And she's not promiscuous! She's a good girl who's struggling to find her way. You-you're a *terrible* stepfather. You should know she needs our support." Jane stood. "I swear, Bolivar, if you do anything to drive Bekah away, it will be the end of me." Letting go of all caution, she said in a trembling voice, "And the end of us."

The shock and powerlessness in his look told her of his despair more clearly than he could possibly have explained in words. He touched her cheek and walked out of the room.

Several weeks after the evening Jane and Bo had argued, Bekah had a bad experience that scared her. She confided to her mother about the special brownies she'd eaten that caused her to black out a couple of times during the evening and effects that lasted far into the morning the following day.

Jane told Bekah about her own experience, the time she had tried pot with a man she dated a long time ago, a man her sister Louise ended up with.

"Really? I don't believe it. You actually smoked pot?"

"I didn't like it. In fact, it was the only time I ever had any."

"So am I forbidden?" Bekah sat on one end of the couch, her mother on the other. It was the middle of summer. On one wall of the living room was a large, light watercolor of lace curtains in an open window blowing outward, on another wall, a painting of a foggy harbor, dark boats in the foreground with their sails furled. Bekah's arms were folded and she faced Jane in the quiet room, still cool, though the day's rising heat was beating down on the house.

"What good would it do?" Jane asked. "Like you couldn't sneak it? I told you my story and what I chose. You know how I feel about it. You're an adult now. And being an adult means you have all kinds of choices to make. You can make foolish choices that cause us to worry about your safety or you can make smart choices, the kind where we won't worry about where you are late at night, whether you're sober or not, or lying in a ditch by the side of the road."

"You sound like Dad and Dolores."

"Uh huh. Am I overseeing the friends you have? Do I make you drink milk five times a day? Do I make you wear some stupid chastity anklet, even though it's worthless if you're stoned out of your mind and some guy decides he wants inside your panties?"

"Mom!"

"You act like I don't know how the world works. Well, I'm just being really honest here. You've never had this kind of talk before without Jesus sitting in on it, so please listen to me. You're putting yourself at risk. But I'll also tell you this: I know you, Bekah. And I absolutely trust that you will choose to do what's best for yourself."

Jane hadn't known she would say the last until the words were out. It was true, though. She knew her daughter was strong and good, and only needed to hear that someone believed in her.

Bekah's eyes widened, as though the foreign concept her mother presented was a hologram that had just walked in through the living room wall. She nodded and said, "I get it, Mom."

The conversation may have contributed to a turning point for Bekah. At the very least, it did make it abundantly clear that she needed to follow the house rules. They were not Rathcreek rules, but they were rules, and she was smart enough not to jeopardize the roof over her head. But more important, she felt loved and cared for, not just her soul, but herself, for who she was.

Bekah made some friends through her job and developed a crush on Ian, the manager at Zumiez. Ian was a skateboarder with a wicked sense of humor who was known as a straight arrow. It was as if fate were giving Bekah a nudge in the right direction. The attitude that had for so long generated the struggles with her Rathcreek parents seemed to fade away as she launched full bore into her new life.

# 6

On the first Sunday in August, Bolivar, Jane, and Bekah drove through the dusty little town of Rathcreek. The dry heat seemed to bake the empty street and its run-down businesses and stores. Inside the car, the air was cool and filled with Billy Joel singing about a heaven for those who wait.

They passed The Fellowship of the Holy Bible located on the main avenue of Rathcreek, and Jane couldn't help but turn to look. She had not seen the familiar building in six years, its narrow stained glass windows, the thin metal cross atop the steeple. Reverend Churlick's flock was pouring out the door of the dark little church into sunlight and the eternal heat to their cars that fairly sizzled in the asphalt lot.

A single life-changing time flooded into her memory. She had been shunned by the church, separated from the abusive husband she would later divorce. She was being counseled by Reverend Logan Churlick. She heard Logan's deep voice, fluid, convincing, as they prayed on their knees in his dim study.

*How convincing he seemed when I was 21,* she thought. *Such a master manipulator.* She recalled the day he counseled her in the way of God's will, and how incapable she was of refusing what he was suggesting. Afterward, when she was at home and had time to reflect, it came to her in mind-numbing clarity that her tryst with a married man twice her age was a horrible mistake.

She sighed, feeling the pang of regret she always felt when recalling the seduction. But she had never regretted her decision to have their twin daughters. He won the paternity suit and legal access to their daughters. For years, Logan held onto his delusion about divorcing Dolores so Jane could join him and together they would be the girls' God-given parents.

She glanced at Bekah and noticed her daughter also gazed out the car's window. Without looking at her mother, she said, "Just checking to see if I can pick out Darcy, but I can't see her."

They continued through town and pulled up to a modest house. Louise sat on her haunches in the morning sunlight flooding the yard. She was staring at the rear of her Plymouth parked on the burnt yellow lawn. She never noticed the car that pulled into the driveway behind her. They piled out of the car and Jane called, "Weeze!"

Louise turned, a sunbreak of a smile on her solemn face. "Hi, Janey, Bo. Oh my God!" She dropped the tool she was carrying. "Bekah! Jumpin' Jesus, you're all grown up!" She galloped over to the driveway and blanketed Bekah in kisses.

Bekah's shyness evaporated in the sloppy, impulsive outburst of affection from her aunt. She giggled and hugged her fiercely.

"What were you working on?" Bo asked.

Louise turned back to her red Plymouth Neon. Rubbing her hands, her sister's family was all but forgotten.

She squatted at the rear of the car, screwdriver in hand. A sliver of a smile appeared.

Louise jammed the screwdriver under the silver letters on the vehicle's back side. Prying at the stubborn metal, she pounded it with the heel of her palm until pieces of paint chipped off. She worked on, pounding, whistling, and occasionally swearing to herself.

Jane, Bo, and Bekah stood watching, mesmerized.

She leaned into a trio of letters until they popped. The letters wobbled, seriously deranged from their original statement on the back of the sports sedan. Louise pried with more might, and the letters suddenly wrenched loose, buckling from the line up. She tossed the screwdriver and grabbed a pair of pliers from the ground.

"Now this is gonna hurt you more'n it hurts me," Louise said, twisting the metal back and forth.

"Aunt Weezie, what're you—"

"Watch," she whispered, voice full of mystery. She gave a furious yank. A portion of the letters popped off, leaving a neat hole in the rear of the vehicle.

With a triumphant "Hah!" she held the *P-l-y* aloft in the pliers and gazed with delight at the letters remaining on the car. "*That's* what I'm talkin' 'bout!"

Bo, Jane, and Bekah broke out in laughter.

When they were inside the house, Joe and Mary Crownhart gave Bekah a wide-armed welcome back into their lives.

"I've missed you!" Bekah said, hugging her Grandma and Grandpa.

"We missed you, too, sweetheart," Mary said, tears shimmering in her eyes. "You've been away for a long time. You're all grown up!"

"Seems like nothing's changed around here, though. It even smells the same," Bekah said. "It's like coming home."

"Hey!" Louise bellowed, striding into the living room. "Did you forget about your Aunt Weezie? I missed you the most, kiddo!"

Bekah hugged her aunt, then pulled back and looked wonderingly at Louise's arms. "Oh man, I love your tats!"

"And I love your pink hair!" Louise said in enthusiastic appreciation.

"I just did it," Bekah said with pride.

Louise, who lived with her parents and had always been on the flip side of conformity, wore her own hair short and spiky.

"I didn't know you had these tattoos," Jane said, coming over to look at her sister's arms. "Are they new?"

"It's my body I.D.," Louise muttered, "In case the CIA tries to take me out."

The CIA was an old story that her mental condition had kept alive over the years.

Louise held no inhibitions about sharing stories with her niece about her life in a town where the largest church was headed by Reverend Logan Churlick. He had shunned her years ago due to her schizophrenia. His faith healing and prayers by parishioners of the Fellowship of the Holy Bible had failed spectacularly, and she relished her outcast status.

"So I said to Carl last time I was in his drugstore, 'You say you won't take money from my hand since I'm shunned, but apparently it doesn't stop you from wanting to poke me.'" She arched her eyebrows. "If you know what I mean."

"Louise!" Joe and Mary said in unison.

Bekah covered her mouth with both hands to stifle her giggle. Jane rolled her eyes, knowing it was fruitless to try to contain Louise.

"Bunch of candy-assed holier-than-thou hypocrites." Louise held up her finger and brought it down, indicating she had scored a point. She nodded and said to her mother's back as she walked into the kitchen, "Just telling it like it is."

Mary and Joe had fallen away from the church years ago when Churlick alienated the girls from not only their mother, but also anyone associated with her, including themselves and Aunt Louise.

"Lunch is ready," Mary said. "And after lunch, maybe we can go through some old photo albums?"

"Sure, Grandma," Bekah said, and took her arm to walk into the dining room together.

❧

As the summer marched on, Bekah's personality came into full bloom. She returned home from her job at the mall one day and walked into the kitchen with what was well on its way to becoming a large gauge ear piercing.

Bolivar was eating a nectarine, bending over the sink while the juice ran down his hand. He turned and saw Bekah's ears. "For cryin' out loud. You realize you look hideous, don't you?"

Jane put her hands on her hips and said, "Great way to start a conversation, Bolivar." She turned to Bekah.

"Honey, you know you don't have to rebel any more, don't you? You are totally accepted."

"Oh yeah?" Bekah bristled. "Doesn't sound like it."

Jane shrank from the challenging tone.

Bolivar finished the piece of fruit and licked his fingers. He turned and faced Bekah. "When you go so counter-culture, you're not only rejecting your dad's values, you're rejecting our way of life, too. Your mother doesn't have any holes in her ears that aren't pin-size, and both of us are completely tattooless."

"It's too late, Bo," Bekah said. "I'm addicted to ink. I can't wait until a couple more paychecks when I'll have enough to get my knuckles tattooed."

Jane's mind reverberated with the remark, which felt like a slap in the face, as if everything she stood for was being rejected by her daughter. She worried about Bekah's new "addiction." Was it simply a replacement for her addiction to God? She gave Bo a look that begged him not to say anything to make things worse.

Bolivar grimaced, shook his head, and muttered, "You can't even stand the same thing for a week, let alone a tattoo for your whole life." He turned to go, saying to Jane, "You deal with her," and left the room.

A part of Jane was troubled to see Bekah hanging her self esteem on tattoos like the students in her high school English classroom whose insecure behaviors screamed, *Look at me! Look at me!* But another deeper part of her saw in Bekah's nonconformity her ability to choose how she would repair and re-create herself. She felt her daughter was rejecting what Logan had taught her about how a woman was supposed to look, and she found a perverse vicarious pleasure in it.

She was savoring her pleasure, when over the horizon of her conscious thought appeared a parable she had taught her students last year about some ancient ceramic cups. The cups were the property of a holy monk, one of the few possessions he permitted himself to keep. Centuries later, when a cup was dropped and broken, even in this condition, it was too precious to destroy. So the cup, which could not be put back in its perfect condition, was repaired with thin seams of gold solder that would hold for centuries to come. The gold solder added a beauty to the cup, making part of its history quite visible.

"Okay, I can see tattoos are your thing. That's fine. But think about this, honey. Someday you may find yourself with a college degree and wanting to walk the halls of power, wanting to change things from the inside. Well, the *establishment* doesn't go for tattoos. You can't cover your knuckles. And so there goes any chance of being hired to a position of influence and being able to work for change."

Bekah's hazel eyes flashed irritation. She folded her arms. "Mom. You need to understand that I've got to make my own way in the world. Which I did against all odds when I was controlled by Dad's Nazi god. If I'm going to be who I'm meant to be, I need to *keep* making my own way."

Jane opened her mouth to respond, then closed it and nodded. She dreaded hearing what Bolivar would have to say when they talked later.

The following day, Bekah came home from Zumiez and found Jane on her knees in the flower bed. She said, "Ian says I should wait on the knuckles. He thinks you're right."

Jane sat back on her haunches, took off her garden gloves, and simply nodded. On the inside, she was ear to ear. She didn't know a lot about Ian, the store manager at Zumiez, who had come to the house for dinner a couple of times, but it gave her a new respect for him. It made her feel safer for Bekah that he seemed to be not only kind hearted, but level headed. She could see that Bekah and Ian were getting pretty chummy.

Month followed month, one season folding into another, and Bekah and Ian fell in love. Bekah's chastity ankle bracelet hit the floor.

Behind closed doors, the arguments between Bo and Jane were heated, and Jane felt as though they could barely communicate anymore without jabs and digs.

"I know you don't care about Bekah's virginity being gone, but that doesn't mean we can't have standards."

"Bo, please—"

"We are not discussing lowering our standards to accommodate a teenage tramp. We need to raise her up to ours," he said.

"Tramp? So now she's a tramp? What do you think Simon's doing up at the university? You think he's still a virgin? If he's anything like his father, he's pretty busy with Lisa or Susie or whatever his date of the week is."

Bolivar's voice was choked with anger. "At least he has the decency to keep it private. We didn't find *him* on the couch last night, did we?"

In the silence that followed, they heard a knock on the door.

Jane opened it.

Bekah stood before them, her expression icy.

*She heard everything*, Jane thought, and a storm of emotion arose in her. *Wait until Bolivar and I are alone again.*

"Before you say anything," Bekah said with a sardonic edge to her voice, "before you make things any worse, let me give you some good news."

Jane looked at Bo, his arms folded.

"Ian and I are moving to Minneapolis. Zumiez corporate is transferring him to open a new store."

Jane could hardly breathe. Losing her daughter again— after one short year, the anger at the harsh judgment Bo leveled against her Bekah but not against his Simon. *I can never forgive Bolivar for being so judgmental.* Her stomach plummeted. *Did Bo cause Bekah to move out?*

"I just wanted to let you know. We'll be leaving next weekend." Bekah turned and left.

Bo came up behind Jane and put his hand on her shoulder. "You need to be grateful for the time you've had with her," he said gently, as if reading her thoughts.

"I know that. But have you thought about how much your—"

"You and Bekah had the time to help each other heal the gaping hole in your lives, and now it's time for her to move on and make her own life. Do you think maybe you're overlooking the major impact you've had on her in one short year? And you'll continue to have an impact. You're her mother again, Jane. Nothing's going to change that." He pulled her around to face him.

Bo's words sank in, the happiness seeping in around the sorrow and anger. Almost against her will, she gave him a small smile. She held up her face and Bo kissed her. The kiss was warm and long and sensuous. She couldn't remember the last time they had kissed so luxuriously; the kiss felt like a relic from the distant past.

She looked into Bo's eyes and thought she saw a spark that he had lost. She held him tightly, choked by the uprushing of love for this man. She cherished the kiss, the spark, and a wave of optimism washed over her telling her she could relax, that Bekah was growing up and leaving home, and it was okay. She and Bo would be okay again, too.

෨

The following weekend, Bekah and Ian stood in the driveway next to their car loaded with the few items they would bring to their new home.

"Oh, Mom, I'm going to miss you so much!" Bekah said, squeezing her eyes against the tears as she hugged Jane.

"I'm going to miss *you!*" Jane replied.

"Got everything?" Bo asked, peering into the window of her car.

Jane and Bo had cosigned on a loan Bekah took out to buy a dependable used car, and Ian and Bekah sold their respective pieces of junk and consolidated all of their belongings in Bekah's reliable Honda. It was packed with a hodge-podge of possessions.

"Wait a minute," Jane said. "I'm going to get a couple of pots and pans to go with the dishes you've already packed to take with you."

"It's okay," Ian said. "Bekah's dad and mom in Rathcreek sent a whole box of kitchenware from Bed, Bath & Beyond to our new address. We're set."

Bekah winced and lowered her head, then directed her gaze at Jane.

Jane's hair stood up on the back of her head and her eyes brimmed with tears. She quickly blinked them away. Her stomach convulsed and her voice came, edged with pain. "You're in touch with your dad and Dolores? You didn't tell me."

"Yeah. They, uh, they contacted me a while ago. We had a long talk and they said they were sorry for whatever they did that made me so unhappy."

"Whatever they *did?*" Jane's heart was pounding.

"Better get on the road," Bolivar said. "You have a long ways to drive."

Jane stared at her husband with an animal ferocity of a mother protecting her young. "You don't care about Logan back in Bekah's life. You just want her out of *our* life."

Bo was poised as if to reply, but instead, leveled her with an acid look. "Leave it alone, Jane," he said and strode off toward the house.

*Of course that would be what you'd say,* Jane thought, heartbroken not only about the danger of the Churlicks once again in her daughter's life, but at the fury that filled her heart where, a short time before, love for Bo had been.

Jane turned back to her daughter. "Bekah! What kind of apology is *that?* It admits no wrong on their part. They're sorry for *whatever?*"

"It is what it is," Bekah said, staring her mother down. "I need to get this whole thing behind me. You do, too, Mom."

Jane nodded, stiffly hugged her daughter and Ian, and walked to the house. With crumpled Kleenex in hand, she watched from the window as Bekah and Ian backed out of the driveway and drove out of her life.

# 7

During the months Bekah and Jane were apart, they grew close. Both mother and daughter had an unquenchable desire to connect because, once again, it was impossible for them to be together.

Emailing regularly, they caught each other up. "Ian just got a raise for the way he put this new store together!" "Bo was nominated for Teacher of the Year and he's having a hard time getting his head through doorways." "I got a kitten and named her Xia. She's adorable, but she ate my favorite plant." "Louise is coming over for a visit and she and I are driving down for the weekend to Portland for some sort of famous foodie event. She's writing a piece about it for *The Stranger*."

They gingerly avoided the topic of Bekah's reconnection with her father and Dolores. Jane was burning to know how close her daughter was to them, how much influence they wielded. But Bekah dropped no hints. Even goaded by her fears, which were substantial, Jane made no inquiries. She would not pump her for information as the Churlicks had. She kept her worries to herself, determined to concentrate on the beautiful relationship that was unfolding with her daughter.

On Mother's Day, flowers arrived and a card came in the mail showing a little girl in a tutu with her hands raised over her head. Jane read what was written inside the card:

> *Mom ~*
>
> *I picked out this card because she reminded me of me. This is the way I remember being when I was little: Free, Happy, Beautiful, and aspiring to be everything. I want you to know that this was the way you let me be and encouraged me to be. You let me love, learn, and explore. Until I left, you were always there, supportive and loving through every-thing. Even though my childhood is now past, you still continuously encourage and love me more than ever. The memories I hold dear to my heart all come from you. And as we grow older together, may we continue on the path that you lovingly set before me as a girl. I love you and cherish every moment.*
>
> *Happy Mother's Day*
> *Love, Bekah*

Jane's eyes teared up. She read the card again, and tears cascaded down her cheeks. While she was reading it aloud to Bo, the phone rang.

"Happy Mother's Day, Mom!"

"Oh, honey, your card is so—so—" Jane choked up and couldn't speak.

"Yeah, I put a lot of thought into that card," Bekah said. "And I mean every word of it. I miss you so much,

Mom. I know we keep in touch with emails and texts—"

"And a phone call here and there."

"Yeah. But you don't know how many times I've thought about sitting on the kitchen counter while you're cooking so I can tell you about everything."

"I know. Cooking just isn't the same without you."

"Oh, and guess what? I have big news."

*You're pregnant*, Jane thought. *Or getting married. God, I hope first married, then pregnant.*

"I found Darcy!"

Jane gasped and her hand went to her heart. "Oh, my God. You found out where she is? How did you find her? Where is she?"

"I've been looking online for some trace of her ever since she cut me off because I was in league with the devil."

"Huh?"

"I mean since I came to live with you, Mom." She giggled.

"Oh, yeah."

"Anyway, I finally found her on the dean's list at a university back east."

This jibed with the 4.0 GPA Bekah told Jane her sister had achieved in high school.

"So which Bible college is it?"

"That's just it, Mom, it's not a Bible college. She's at the University of Massachusetts at Amherst."

"No way. A secular university?" A jolt of hope shot through Jane, driving her to wild scenarios of reconciliation. *If Darcy isn't attending a Bible college, she's not being influenced by church people, by Logan. She's all the way across the country. Could this mean things are strained between them?*

"Yup. And I'm going to get in touch with her."

"Of course. A call?"

"No, I'm flying to Boston, staying with Simon. He said I can borrow his car to drive from Boston to Amherst."

Bekah's stepbrother was a student at Tufts University and his serious girlfriend, Joy, a graduate student in economics at Harvard. It was a complete fluke that they should be pursuing their education in the same state in which Darcy had chosen to go to school.

"That's right. Simon and Joy are in Boston. That's perfect." Jane looked out the window of the kitchen at the profusion of flowers bursting with color in the garden. The sky was a bright blue, but she knew the image could be deceptive. Mays in Berry Valley were known for their icy winds accompanying a clear blue sky.

"It's the only way," Bekah said. "I've thought about it a lot. I don't want her to have a chance to hang up on me. She needs to see me standing there when she opens the door, to know that I've come across the country to ask her to let me back into her life."

It was a bold plan. A risky plan. Darcy would be resistant. Otherwise, this far into the school year, away from the influence of Logan and Dolores, she would have already contacted Bekah. Jane swallowed around the lump in her throat.

"Well, honey, I support you a hundred percent. You know that. Go get your sister!"

Bekah flew to Boston. She spent the night on Simon and Joy's couch. The next morning, with clammy hands, she drove Simon's car to the university.

She pulled into one of the large parking lots and sat there. She had never been on a college campus before, and Amherst was immense.

*I have no idea where to start.* She spread out the campus map she had printed the night before, studied it for several minutes. *I can't even find the parking lot I'm in.*

"Well, this is pointless." She folded the map, stuck it in her purse, and locking the car, headed toward what she hoped would be the center of campus.

Bekah walked up to the first person she met, a studious-looking young woman carrying books and walking fast.

"Uh, excuse me. Can you tell me—"

The student kept walking, eyes on her cell phone, thumbs tapping a message.

Bekah sighed. *This isn't going to be easy.*

She headed toward a stately brick building and walked inside. Three students meandered through the wide hallway lined with doors.

"Excuse me," Bekah said to a young man reading a bulletin board.

"Yeah?" He took his eyes from the job postings and looked at her with the eyes of someone who's been interrupted but doesn't particularly mind.

"I was wondering if you could tell me if there's a directory that lists students' dorm rooms."

"Not that I know of. That's a privacy thing, you know. Security. Who you looking for?"

"My sister, Darcy Churlick."

"Don't know her," he said. "Have you tried the quad café?"

"No. Where's that?"

He walked out the door and pointed to a building that seemed at least a quarter mile away. "It'll be lunch time soon. Maybe she'll be there."

"Thanks," she said and waved good-bye.

She got lost once, ended up totally turned around, and talked to three more students as she walked through campus. Eventually, she found the quad where a few stragglers remained at the tables.

"Excuse me."

"Yes?" A tall black woman with hair tumbling down her back turned to face Bekah.

"I'm looking for my sister. Her name is Darcy Churlick. Do you know her?"

The woman eyed Bekah skeptically. "She didn't tell you how to find her room, or which building she's in?"

"Uh, she told me, but I forgot. I didn't write it down."

"Can't you call her?" she said, picking up her tray.

"Um, well, my phone's broken."

"Do you know her number? There's phones over there if it's on campus you're calling."

Bekah was silent a moment. "I don't know her number. You know, I just push a button to call her."

"Uh huh. Well, I don't know her. I wish you luck." And she took her tray toward the exit.

Bekah's stomach growled. *Oh man, I'm hungry.* She dug in her purse and eyed the dollar and change she found in her wallet. *Shit. Didn't think about lunch. Stupid!* She looked over one shoulder, then the other, and glanced at the time on her cell phone, then quickly slipped it back into her purse.

She bought a Snickers at a machine in the hallway, tore the package open, and gnawed on it like a famished child in one of her father's World Vision posters. *What the hell was I thinking? This was a stupid idea. Stupid! I'm an idiot for thinking I could track her down in a school this size.*

Bekah left the quad when she had imposed on the remaining few students without success. She walked into the fading afternoon. She had spent almost the entire day asking questions of random students.

"Oh my God, this sucks," she said, peering at a massive brick and glass building nearby. She walked a little farther and spun slowly around, gazing at unfamiliar red brick buildings with gabled roofs surrounding her.

*I don't even know how to get back to the lot where my car is parked. Simon's car.* A sinking feeling almost made her cry.

She walked by one building, and another, aware that soon it would be early evening, not late afternoon, and she would be completely and totally lost—in the dark. She found herself looking up at a multi-story building she figured, by the window adornments, was a dorm. She went inside and, seeing a pretty Asian student wearing glasses who was slung over a large chair reading a book, she sighed. She walked over to her and asked about her sister.

"You're Darcy's sister? Oh yeah, I know Darcy," the young woman said. "I didn't know she had a sister. But she's not in this dorm."

"Oh, thank God! I am so freakin' lost, my cell phone is broken, and I don't even know where my car is parked anymore."

The student stood up. "I'm Amber. Here, let me take you to her dorm. It's sort of hard to find from here."

Soon, they were standing outside Darcy's dorm room. Out a window at the end of the hall, Bekah could see dusk was setting in.

"It's a surprise," Bekah said.

Amber moved to one side. She folded her arms in the pose of someone anticipating the scene about to unfold.

Heart pounding, Bekah rapped on the door.

The door opened and Darcy stood there. Her eyes widened when she saw Bekah. She took a step backward and her hand went to the doorknob.

"Darcy! It's me," Bekah said, smiling uneasily. She took a step forward.

Darcy glared at her with hands extended. "Stop! No! No way!"

Amber's eyes were round with shock.

"C'mon, sissy," Bekah said. "Please! I flew all the way out here from Minnesota."

Bekah recognized with dismay Darcy's look as akin to one from her childhood when she had stared at the first dead creature they'd ever seen, a half-eaten bird lying in the yard. Darcy stepped back inside her room and slammed the door.

"Well, I've done my good deed for the day," said Amber. "I think I'll go creep back under a rock." She turned and hurried down the hallway.

Bekah hardly heard her. She stared at the door, frozen to the worn hall carpet. She felt like she might throw up.

Darcy's voice broke through from the other side of the door. "Go away! I'm not coming out. I don't want to see you."

Tears streaming, Bekah let out a savage yowl of a cry. She beat at the door.

A minute later, Darcy's roommate came out.

"Uh, I'm sorry to have to tell you that Darcy said she absolutely doesn't want to see you. She's calling campus security right now." The dark haired young woman in big square glasses looked embarrassed.

"Campus security?" she said. "What the *fuck?!*"

The roommate stepped back, blinking. "I'm supposed to tell you that Darcy not only refuses to see you, but— uh—she'll never see you."

Bekah's crying broke loose, her hunched shoulders shuddering. She turned and walked blindly toward the stairs at the end of the hall where a security guard was heading toward her.

Most of the following couple of hours was spent in the security guard's vehicle cruising parking lots, trying to locate Bekah's car.

That evening at Simon and Joy's apartment, Bekah received an email from Darcy saying she felt violated by the sneak attack and she never wanted to see her again. For the second time that day, uncontrollable tears flowed.

In the morning, Bekah returned home to the small apartment she shared with Ian in Minnesota. Her heart was broken.

# 8

A few months after Bekah's trip to Massachusetts, Jane received a phone call.

"First of all, everything's okay," Jane's father's voice came over the phone.

"What? What is it?!" Jane asked.

"Your mother's got a heart issue and is going to be having surgery tomorrow."

"Tomorrow? A heart issue? Did she have a heart attack? Stroke? What, Dad?" Jane's own heartbeat was in her ears and she sounded louder than she meant to be.

"Calm down, Janey. She was having some issues, got an EKG test, and the doc said she needed a stent or two to open up a couple of clogged blood vessels. It's scheduled for tomorrow at 10:30."

"The surgery? She's having surgery tomorrow?"

"Well, I think the doc said it's a procedure. Tomorrow. At Sacred Heart in Spokane. I thought you'd want to know."

"Yes," she said, closing her eyes. "Of course I want to know. Thanks so much for calling, Dad. I'll be there."

"Who's having surgery tomorrow?" Bolivar asked when Jane clicked off her phone.

"My mom is having 'a stent or two' put in tomorrow morning at 10:30," Jane said, going online to find out what a stent was. "Here it is. Balloon angioplasty and stents."

She read for a few minutes, her fingertips to her bottom lip. "It's a common surgery, but there can be complications. They snake a catheter up to the blood vessel near her heart through an incision in the groin and then inflate the balloon that's attached to the catheter where there's a blockage to compress the plaque against the blood vessel wall. Then they put the stent in to keep it held back."

"You don't want me with you, do you?" said Bolivar.

"Yes. No. I don't know. I don't want you to miss too much school if Mom needs me. I might decide to stay for a week or more. I should go alone."

Bolivar nodded. "Let me call the sub service to arrange for someone to cover your classes for the next few days anyway. We can always tack on more days, if you decide to stay longer."

Jane studied his eyes, his voice. *Is he glad I'm going alone? He looks relieved.* The possibility sent a shock through her. She scolded herself for over-reacting. Still, her gut told her she had seen something.

*Since Bekah moved to Minneapolis, we haven't been close, not the way we used to be. He's been so edgy, distracted. And I've been a real witch at times.*

She had thought the tension between them would dissipate once Bekah was out of the house. But they were still bickering, and it seemed she could do nothing right. She found herself resenting his domineering manner, the way he treated her like one of his students. It came to her then.

She was relieved Bo would not be with her on her trip to Rathcreek. She was looking forward to the break from him as much as he needed time away from her.

"That's right. I'd better put together some sub plans for the next few days. I'll email them to the office and they can get them to the sub." She went to the bedroom to pack her suitcase.

Mary Crownhart came through the surgery without any trouble. Later that day, when the effects of the anesthetic wore off, Jane was waiting, along with her father and sister in the room Mary was wheeled into on the Cardiac Unit.

"Okay, I gotta go now, Bekah," Jane said into her phone. "Yes, I'll tell her you send your love."

Jane's mother, in a blue print gown, was transferred to her bed and tucked under covers by a nurse, who attached intravenous lines that ran from her arms to clear plastic bags full of liquid. Once she made sure Mary was comfortable, she left her with her family.

Mary, who everyone had always thought so healthy, seemed alien in a hospital bed. She wore no make-up and her hair was pulled back into a pony tail. A machine monitoring her heart beeped rhythmically.

Jane and Louise were on one side of the bed, their father on the other. Jane took her mother's hand and held it to her lips. "Oh, Mom. We're so glad you're okay."

"I feel a little groggy still, but great," Mary said, the words drawn out slowly. "Isn't it amazing that once they clear you out, you feel instantly better?"

"You look good!" said Louise. "Now you won't need to have the CIA out for a layin' on of hands."

Joe frowned at Louise, then leaned over and gave Mary a kiss on her forehead. She smiled at him and then looked placidly at her girls.

He said, "Louise, you know that man will never darken our door again. Not after what he did to Janey."

"Thank the Magic God!" Louise said, a little too loudly, laughed, and winked at her sister. Jane smiled and nodded. *Magic God Fail.*

Jane squeezed Mary's hand. "Bekah sends her love from Minnesota."

Mary nodded, smiled. "So glad she's come back to us."

Jane couldn't take her eyes off her mother. It felt as though she had never really seen her, as if she'd been look-ing at Mary all her life through a screen that separated them. She found herself speculating about the surgery. What if it hadn't gone well? What if something unthink-able had happened? What if Mary's goodness and grace were no longer a part of Jane's world?

*We've been through so much together,* Jane thought, *including the worst mistake of my life. But I'd never un-do it. Two adorable babies and my break with the church are the best things that ever happened to me.*

Bo came to mind. Jane had often said Bo was the best thing that had ever happened to her. His love had rescued her at the lowest point of her life—when she had lost her children. Where would she be without him? She didn't blame him for not wanting to be with her.

*It's like we're strangers, trying to find something to connect us. Without catastrophe, there's nothing to hold us together. We're just grasping at air. Why can't he stand by me, now that Bekah has re-connected with Logan? I need him. I feel so alone.*

Mary stood by Jane when she divorced Jake. She quietly sided with Jane's desperate need to end her abusive marriage, even though Mary knew she was going against church teachings. She stood by Jane when she battled with Churlick for her girls. Eventually, Mary dropped out of the church, and while the act of defiance riled her husband at first, he finally came to his daughter's defense and joined Mary in the boycott. By the act, Mary had taught her daughter that love was the highest of all commandments, and living a life focused on love was the highest form of living.

The thought sent a small shiver through Jane's shoulders. She thought of her struggles with Bo. She would try harder—if it wasn't already too late. She would reach out to Bo and make him love her again the way he used to.

She whispered, "I love you so much, Mom. I can never thank you enough for standing by me." She looked up. "You, too, Dad."

Eyes closed, her mother gave her a wan smile. Joe gave her a curt nod.

When Mary was released from the hospital the following day, Jane settled into her old bedroom and tended to her mother with the kind of care she had lavished on her children when they were sick. Louise, who had always lived with her parents, welcomed Jane's help and took care of her mother as well, in her own inimitable way.

"Thought I'd cheer you up with some news," Louise said, bringing in a tray with breakfast on it.

Jane followed and placed a vase with a daisy in it on the tray.

"You didn't need to fix me breakfast in bed. You two are such spoilers!" Mary smoothed her sheets and sat up in bed. "What news, honey?"

Louise set the tray on her mother's lap. Steam rose from a cup of tea and a plate of scrambled eggs. Two pieces of toast, slathered in bright red jam and cut in an abstract shape of hearts, lay beside them.

Looking like the trickster she was, Louise said, "Well, Dallas said to me last night that I reminded him of his second wife."

"Second?" Jane said. "I thought he'd only been married once before. How many wives has he had?"

Louise hung her head, her impish giggle getting the best of her. She took a moment to collect herself, then, suppressing a smile, said, "One."

*One?* Jane let out a shriek. "Louise! Congratulations!" She threw her arms around her sister.

"Oh, honey," Mary said. Her brows were drawn up in concern, but they relaxed in a moment. "I'm very happy for you."

Louise took in a deep breath and nodded as a slow smile spread across her face. "It's been a long time comin'— but I say better late than never."

"Does Dallas want kids?" Mary asked, keeping her eyes on the eggs she was piling onto her fork.

"Hell no," Louise answered. "And you know I'm not the mothering type, even though I'm one helluva good aunt to Jane's kids."

"He has a couple of kids from his first marriage, right?" Jane said.

"Yeah, but they're all grown up and away at college, so he doesn't get to see them as often as he'd like."

Mary patted her hand. "You deserve happiness, Louise. I like Dallas. He's just the type of guy to keep you on your toes. He'll take care of you."

*A cyclone in a Santa suit,* Jane mused, resurrecting a long-ago memory from when she and Dallas had dated. *Louise is perfect for him.*

By Sunday, Jane's father shooed her home, saying she needed to get back to her classroom and he could handle Mary's care with the help of Louise.

The morning Jane packed her suitcase, she was in the grip of a wild idea that would not let go. She turned to Louise's closet and pulled out a dress with large, bright flowers on it. Holding the dress up to herself, she said, "Can I borrow this, Weez?"

Her sister nodded. "Sure."

"What would you think if I told you I was going to drop in on the Fellowship on my way out of town?"

Louise broke into a fit of laughter, covering her mouth with a hand, only wickedly gleeful eyes showing.

"Gonna do some undercover work? Beat Churlick at his own game?" she asked, rubbing her hands together.

Jane's eyes were bright. "I'm going to see if I can get Darcy back."

# 9

Jane arrived late, snuck into the back of the church, and sat down in a low, hard pew. The familiar odors of mold, wood polish, and perspiration closed in on her.

Dolores was no longer the lone instrumentalist at her piano, but was joined by a guitarist and drummer. Other than that, it was much the same as when Jane had been a member a couple of decades ago.

Somewhere in the middle of his sermon, Logan Churlick noticed her in the back of the church. He froze, and the color drained from his face. He tripped on what he was saying, after which there was a paralyzed pause. In a moment, he made himself continue as if he'd simply swallowed wrong.

Afterward, Jane waited for him in the foyer of the church.

"Hello, Logan," she said, walking up to him.

Dolores was at his side.

He nodded his greeting, saying nothing, glancing furtively at Dolores. Parishioners milled around them.

He had aged in the six years since she had last seen him. His hair, once so vigorously black, was now peppered with gray. Tall and imposing, he was still handsome for a man old enough to be her father. And he still had the commanding black eyes. Where before there had been a web of lines around his smiling eyes, now the lines around his eyes and creasing his forehead were more pronounced.

Jane caught her breath at the sight of Dolores. *Holy shit! She looks pretty good—for a she-wolf.*

Reverend Churlick's wife had always been mousy in the past, with her nondescript hair, the little girl voice, the rounded shoulders. Her hair was held back with an ornate clip. Not a wisp of gray. She had always appeared powerless against her husband's power. Now, she lifted her chin and gazed at Jane with barely concealed contempt.

Logan and Jane stared at one another for several seconds, then he said, "I find it hard to believe you are brazen enough to show up here."

"I'm here."

Again, a prolonged silence. Jane looked into his intense black eyes, trying to read them. Once, they had seemed to hold a depth of understanding, ages of understanding.

"Don't you think we should talk, Logan?"

"Let me tell you something—" Dolores said in her high-pitched voice.

Logan cut her off with a look. Then he bent and whispered something in her ear. She fixed him with accusing eyes, crossed her arms, and said, "They're my children, too."

Logan slumped in defeat, as if they'd had this conversation in the past.

He pressed his lips together and turned to face Jane. "I know what you're up to. I know you and Bekah were in Boston trying to locate Darcy."

"What? I was never in Boston with Bekah."

"We *know* you were the one behind her being there," Dolores said.

"What are you talking about?"

"You were the one who found out where Darcy was and sent Bekah, trying to use her to get to Darcy," Logan said.

Jane raised her voice, which was sure to be heard by the people around them in the foyer. "For your information, Bekah has been looking on the Internet, trying to find her sister, ever since she came to live with me. She finally found her because Darcy was listed on the dean's list. It had nothing to do with me. Did it ever occur to you that Bekah loves and misses her sister and wants, more than anything, to have a relationship with her?"

Without skipping a beat, Logan said, "Well I want a relationship with Bekah, too, but she won't have anything to do with me ever since Boston—and that letter *you* wrote for her."

"Letter? What letter?" Jane felt as though she had gone down a rabbit hole. Then she put it together. *After her trip to Boston, Bekah must've written a letter. She must've cut them off! She told me she was really pissed at whatever he was still telling Darcy to keep them apart.*

"I never wrote any letter."

"Really." He said the word in a tone that was not a question but an accusation. "Then you just told her what to say."

"Can't Bekah do something on her own without you putting me in the middle of it?"

His black eyes flashed. "We tried to call, but she wouldn't answer. We wrote letters to her, but she never wrote back. You've told Bekah that her own father is poison."

Again, the feeling of disorientation. No way had she written the letter he was accusing her of penning for Bekah. Then, it hit her. *They think I'm capable of turning Bekah against them because it's what they would do—what they've done.*

Logan's voice was close to breaking. "It's true, isn't it? Bekah won't have anything to do with us because you've brainwashed her against us."

"*Me?*" she said. "You brainwashed Darcy and Bekah against me for years. Told them I wasn't a Christian. How could you do such a thing? You *baptized* me, Logan. Even if I'm not a Christian, you have to be pretty sick to turn my daughters against me."

People in the foyer were staring at them.

Logan looked around at his parishioners and suggested to Jane they go outside where their discussion would not be quite so public.

"No way!" Jane raised her voice. "Let's have this out right here, right now. And what about when you told the girls that every birthday I would call them and then hang up? What was that about? I never called them." She faced them, hands on hips.

"So she told you that," Dolores said, eyes narrowing. "We know it was you."

"I swear I never called them. *Never!*"

Logan's voice was certain. "Then you had someone else do it."

The warped world he and Dolores had created enveloped Jane like a scene out of Wonderland. There was no truth she could offer for which they didn't have an immediate fictionalized counterpoint. She marveled at a reality where lies were woven thick enough to block out the light of the real world.

Suddenly, she wondered why she had thought this confrontation would yield anything. What had she been thinking? There was only the thinnest ray of hope that she could influence the Churlicks. They would never agree to the girls getting in touch—because it could destroy the web of lies that held Darcy.

So here Jane was again, attempting to reason with Logan. She should have known better. She had learned over the years that reasoning with him was like trying to grab at a gaseous substance that, besides being a waste of time, always left its stink. Once again, they were locked in conflict; once again, she was unable to change anything.

She said, "Look, we're not getting anywhere. You keep coming up with so-called facts that have nothing to do with what really happened. I've *never* pursued the girls while they were with you. I'm smart enough to know it was fruitless, that it had to come from them." Jane paused, then took a path she knew would get them back on track. "You say you want a relationship with Bekah?"

Dolores exclaimed, "Of course! I love my daughters, and no matter how much you've turned her against me, I will always love Bekah."

Dolores' words hit Jane hard in her gut. *Your daughters? I just want to rip your stupid face off.*

Over the years, being mother to her husband's illegitimate children had become more than security for Dolores in her marriage; she had developed feelings for her adopted daughters. But Dolores had never realized what she had done. In order for her to be mother to the twins, they first had to be brainwashed so they could be ripped away from Jane.

Jane shoved her anger down. "I'm here to get these girls back together."

Logan goaded her. "Yes, and then you could put your hooks into Darcy. Well, we're not giving her up. You gave the girls to us because it was financially convenient at the time, and now you want Darcy back. What kind of mother does that?" Some of the old hurt was in his voice, the terrible anguish of the day she had stepped out of her children's life, and his.

Dolores heard it, too. In a voice filled with scorn, she said, "I would have *never* given up my children. And I'll tell you right now, you're never getting *my daughter* from me!"

Her words stunned Jane. Before she could think, her hands tighten into fists. She stepped forward.

Logan moved between the women, as if to keep Jane from throwing herself at Dolores. He took Jane's wrists.

She looked into Logan's black eyes, saw the fear. She held his gaze and said in a heated whisper, "What the hell? You grab me like I'm out of my mind for wanting my own daughter? While your wife, the home wrecker, says she's going to keep Darcy from me? You've got to be joking."

With all her might, she yanked her wrists down and broke free.

"You stole my daughters, you goddamn bitch! You and Logan. I should scratch both your eyes out."

Logan did not take his eyes off her. Dolores' mouth fell open.

Parishioners around them gaped in silence, except for a boy who stared at her. He turned to his mother. "Is that lady going to hell? She took God's name in vain."

Trembling with rage, Jane gazed at the boy. The absurdity in the boy's question hit her full on, knocking the rage on end. Laughter bubbled up out of her. The laughter fed on the warped reality inside this church that had nothing to do with real life. It was a while before she got herself under control.

She looked around at the people, the Churlicks huddled together, and took a deep breath. Looking at the ceiling, she pushed her hair behind her ear. *I'm going to give it one more shot—for Bekah and Darcy.*

"Let's just get through this, can we? We need to come to some sort of agreement. Not for you or me, but for the girls."

Logan said in a fervent voice, "Well, I'll tell you right now, you can't use my daughters to jerk me around anymore."

The irony almost sent Jane reeling into another fit of laughter. She steadied herself. "I'm jerking *you* around? You convinced our girls that I was under the influence of Satan and demons."

"You gave them up. You have no one to blame but yourself."

Images flashed through her mind. For almost a year of hatred from Bekah and Darcy she had hung on, had fought fiercely, until the day she found a note from one of the girls saying she wanted to kill Jane.

Logan folded his arms and said, "I would've thought that a good mother would do whatever it took to keep her children."

"All right. Let's cut this short, Logan. You say I've brainwashed Bekah, and I say you've brainwashed Darcy. So let's do something that might just heal this family once and for all. Let's send both of them to a deprogrammer."

Logan's face flushed and no words came from his open mouth. He had no answer to pull out of the air.

After a moment, he drew himself up and said, "I have no intention of doing any such thing. Darcy is an adult, and she has a mind of her own. But I can tell you this: she'd never agree to do such a thing."

*Of course she wouldn't, because you've brainwashed her!*

"Bekah has a mind of her own, too," Jane said. "But for the sake of healing this family, I'll talk to Bekah. And you can talk to Darcy. Bekah respects my opinion, and would go to a deprogrammer if I asked her to, especially if it meant she would get her sister back in her life. Don't you think Darcy would respect your judgment if you talked to her about it?"

Logan shook his head, impassive. "She can see fine on her own. In fact, she just had Lasik surgery on her eyes a week ago. Heh, heh, heh."

The news of Darcy's eye surgery did not amuse Jane. She wanted to plead with him, but held her voice steady. "Don't you think it's worth a try? What's the worst that can happen? If Darcy is *not* brainwashed as you say, then nothing will change. If she *is*, then it can be addressed and the twins can have each other in their lives again."

Logan said, "You can send Bekah to a deprogrammer, but I have no intention of talking to Darcy."

Jane sighed, depleted of whatever good will was driving her on behalf of Bekah and Darcy. "Got it. I'm out of here. We have nothing more to talk about."

She turned and headed toward the door, parting the rapt audience surrounding them. She got into her Subaru, and pointed the car toward home.

On the road, she let out a shaky breath. "Jesus Christ. What *was* that?"

She couldn't help going over and over the conversation, the shock still lingering from the barrage leveled at her. She went over her part in the melee, biting her lip.

*Send both girls to a de-programmer? How could I be so stupid as to think I could talk with Logan and Dolores and they would agree to do what was best for the girls? They can't see what's best for the girls, only what's best for them. Salvation trumps everything.*

Jane wondered if she should call Bolivar. The scene in the church was too much to bear on her own. She needed to share the weight of it. She pulled over before getting onto I-90 and called Bolivar on her cell, slipping the phone into the hands-free device.

"How's your mom doing? Where are you?" His voice was smooth and deep.

The sound of it soothed her nerves.

"I'm on my way home."

She sighed, reading from his tone that things seemed normal between them. Assuming he missed her, she suddenly missed him, missed his humor whose irony always brought her perspective and solace. She wondered briefly if she had imagined the strain between them.

After relating the state of her mother's health, Jane confessed she had just come from Logan's church. She gave herself over completely to the humiliating defeat she had experienced and shared the highlights of her conversation with the Churlicks.

"You're shittin' me."

"No, I am not," she answered and signaled to merge onto the interstate heading west. "They are amazingly accomplished at coming up with crazy explanations for anything they've convinced themselves is true, even when confronted with what really happened. They were able to pluck reason after cock-eyed reason out of thin air to back up their paranoid views. It was surreal."

He whistled.

"Dolores said she would've never given up *her* children. And she was never going to let me have *her* daughter." Jane's voice was thick and a lump came to her throat at the memory.

"That bitch."

"I could hardly hold it together—" she paused, "but Logan stepped between us and—"

"He what?"

"Yeah, I think he may have stopped me from actually attacking Dolores. In front of everyone in the church foyer. Uh, needless to say, I wasn't myself."

She flicked on the turn signal. Passing a logging truck, she told Bo about her suggestion that they talk the girls into seeing a de-programmer. "I could see it was a lost cause—so I just took my shell-shocked self and limped out of there."

The phone was silent. Then Bo said, "Sometimes I lose sight of what you've been through. There are times when you drive me absolutely crazy and I can hardly stand to be in the same room with you—"

Jane caught her breath. Tears blurred her vision. She blinked them back. A sharp ache stirred at the memory of their recent clashes. *What is he saying? Is this what he's been thinking about while I've been away?*

"Then you go and do something like this." He drew in a long breath, exhaled. "You know and I know things haven't been right with us for a while. Ever since Bekah. Actually, since before Bekah. I just want you to know that even though you're sorta impossible to live with, you're my hero."

"Your hero? But I'm impossible to live with? What the hell does that mean?"

"You're the most courageous person I know. Going into the den of the lion and . . . But let's talk about where we're at when you get home. I'm sorry I brought it up over the phone."

The next six hours on the freeway west were torture. If she thought her confrontation with the Churlicks was stressful, the doubts Bolivar had expressed were pure agony for her.

After hours of driving and hours of worry, Jane arrived at home, exhausted. She found Bo in the kitchen with the light off. He stood when she entered. Mindless of anything but her need for comfort, she walked into his tentative embrace, looked up at his hesitant smile.

He let go of her and stepped back, eyes roaming the cold, dusky kitchen. He flipped on the light and returned to his seat at the table where his tea sat before him.

"Tea?"

She shook her head.

He motioned her to a seat facing him and when she had settled into the chair, he cleared his throat. "I'm sorry to pile this on top of all the other stuff you're dealing with. I love you, Jane, but I just don't know how to handle your moodiness, your hair-trigger anger anymore."

*Oh my God. He's*—She couldn't finish the thought. She was bewildered, as if what Bolivar voiced was a shock to hear, even though a part of her had feared such a pronouncement for some time. But her stubborn, selfish heart would not hear it, would hear nothing but her own pain. She was helpless to argue with this attack by the one man who had always stood by her. Her eyes welled with tears. Her throat tightened and she couldn't find her voice.

"Jane, listen. Neither of us is happy. Haven't been happy in a long time. I'm just the one who's stating the obvious. It's not healthy to bicker the way we do. I just can't handle it anymore."

"*You* can't handle it? What kind of man says that when his wife's mother just went through heart surgery? What kind of husband turns away when his wife's tangled up in the toughest fight of her life—dealing with the worst excuse for a human being over the possibility of getting her kid back?"

Bo crossed his arms, his look glazed over. Then, as if he couldn't endure one more word of bickering, he turned away from her to the window where the barest of light in the evening sky still shone.

She said through clenched jaws, "Through good times and bad, through sickness and health. What a sorry excuse for a husband you are!"

"That's right. Turn it all on me."

The look on Bo's face chilled her heart. The look said there was no reason to fight for their love; he had nothing to lose. "You think you're such a victim. You're so blind, you can't see anything but the pain your daughters put you through. Any emotion I might have doesn't even enter into the picture. You love nothing but your precious girls. Everything you used to value is trash to you now. Me? Simon? We're nothing but *reminders* to you. You resent us because we have what you lost."

"That's not true!"

He continued as if he hadn't heard her. "You are so emotionally distant. No, no, you are emotionally locked away. We used to do this beautiful dance when we cooked in the kitchen together. We'd move around each other, you chopping and me sautéing. You'd walk by and pat my butt or I'd pat yours. We'd smile at each other, feeling the love. There is no playful touch any more.

"When I'd drive the truck to go get some manure in the spring, you were there right along with me to get some flowers for the yard. You used to buckle up right next to me. Now you sit by the window."

"Well, you moved away from me, too."

Bo's expression was tender, ironic. "Where does the driver move to?"

Jane hung her head, her gaze focused on hands folded in her lap.

"You used to let me comfort you, in fact, you counted on me to help you through rough times to do with your girls. Now you shut me out. You turn your back to me, don't talk. You keep it all inside."

"You don't understand. You can't understand what I'm going through. It doesn't help to be comforted on the outside when you're bleeding to death on the inside."

He scraped back his chair and rose, planting both hands on the table. He shook his head. "You are not the same girl I married. You are so bitter it's like living with a PTSD time bomb that's blasted apart the last shred of love I had for you."

The words took Jane's breath away. *He doesn't love me anymore!*

The effort of collecting her thoughts left her feeling dizzy. A crack began inside her, widened, and bits of her crumbling heart fell in. Tears sprang to her eyes and ran down her cheeks. The void left behind by Bolivar's abandonment terrified her. Terror turned to anger, and she heard herself speaking as if from a place far away.

"Go, then! Get the hell away from me and don't come back!" she shouted. "I hate you, you coward!"

When he slammed the back door, the windows rattled. She stood in the kitchen alone, shuddering, still reeling from an anger beyond her ability to control, which suddenly turned into racking sobs.

# 10

Evasive conversations with Bekah over the phone did not hint at the wreckage of Jane's life. When her daughter asked to speak to Bo, Jane claimed he was not available or out with friends. Mortified and depressed when her husband packed up and moved out of their home, she could not bear to share the state of affairs with Bekah.

A week after Jane's run-in at the church with the Churlicks, Bekah called late one night.

"Mom, are you sitting down?"

"Bekah," she said, rubbing her eyes "I'm lying down. It's almost midnight. Everything okay?"

"Yes!" she said in an excited voice. "Darcy contacted me!"

"You're kidding!"

"No, I'm not kidding. Somehow, she saw that I loved and missed her, and I was just trying to get in touch to get her back in my life."

*However they twisted our conversation, it was relayed to Darcy by Logan and Dolores. She somehow put it together.*

Jane blinked back tears of joy. "I am thrilled for you, sweetheart!"

"Listen to this," Bekah said.

> *Dear Bekah,*
>
> *I heard from Mom and Dad what happened with Jane at church. Even though it was lies upon lies, I figured out one thing and I hope it's true: it was you, not Jane, who was behind your wanting to see me again. And after some soul searching, I had to admit to myself that I missed you, too. There's nothing closer than twins, right? I figured it was up to me to contact you and judge for myself if you are acting on your own or not.*
>
> *Write me back, sissy.*
> *Love, Darcy*

The twins' email reunion almost ended before it began. In her second email, Darcy told Bekah that she would refuse to communicate with her any further if she mentioned Jane.

Bekah chafed at the restrictions her sister imposed and resented her setting the rules. Guilt made it difficult to play the game her sister was asking her to play. Yet she could understand Darcy's fear of dealing with their strange shared past. She also recognized that her relationship with her twin came before anything else. Once they were strongly reunited, she hoped Darcy would see a way to reconcile with their mother.

After weeks of emails, the twins graduated to the long phone calls of people who miss each other and can't bear to hang up. Finally, Darcy traveled to Minnesota for a weekend with her sister.

Like pieces of the Berlin Wall, the barrier of faith keeping the twins suspicious and separated for years fell away to reveal the deep love buried beneath the concrete of belief and the razor wire of fear. The reunion was a joyful, almost desperate coming together of two parts of a whole.

"I can't believe you're actually here." Bekah's arms were clamped tightly around her sister, as if she would never let her go.

"I missed you so much, Sissy!" Darcy let herself be engulfed by her sister's embrace. She held onto Bekah while underground emotions she didn't know she had moved her to tears.

Ian brought in Cokes on a tray. He set the tray on a crate that served as a coffee table in their apartment. "Here," he said, placing a box of tissues beside the tray. "I'll get dinner going."

The twins talked long into the night, catching up, comparing lives. Long after Ian went to bed, they sat next to each other on the second-hand couch that filled the small living room.

"So what made you change your mind about seeing me?" Bekah asked.

Darcy was silent a moment. She pulled at a loose thread in the cushion. "I don't know. I guess it was when Dad and Mom said something about you coming to Massachusetts by yourself."

"That's right. So?"

"So I decided to take a chance. I had to see for myself that you weren't there because Jane was manipulating you, trying to get to me through you."

Bekah shook her head, let out a long breath. "It was me. All alone. I just wanted to see you so bad. I saved up some money and flew all the way from here to Massachusetts. I stayed with Simon and Joy. They let me use their car to drive out to the university. I'd been looking for some trace of you online for two years."

"Really?"

"Yes, really. Good thing you're such a smarty pants. If you weren't on the dean's list, I would never have known. I figured you were at some Bible college in Kansas City or something."

Darcy giggled. "No. A degree from that kind of college doesn't get you a decent job. And I intend to get a very good job."

"And something in you wanted to be independent, so you went about as far from Rathcreek as you could."

"Maybe. I don't know why you're not speaking to Mom and Dad, but I'm still close to them."

"Here's the thing. I know we were told Jane, I mean Mom, would try to get to us, turn us against them. But that's ridiculous, considering six years of turning us against her. I'm having a hard time accepting what they did that wrecked our life with our mom."

"I can't listen to this." Darcy stood up. "I've got to pee. I wish you'd call her Jane like we always have. In fact, I don't want to hear about her at all. She's not my mom."

Bekah watched her sister's back as she walked down the narrow hallway to the bathroom.

At the end of the weekend, Bekah and Darcy were sleep deprived. Bekah abided by her sister's rule to not mention Jane. When they parted, they vowed to never let anything come between them again.

∽

When Jane learned from Bekah that Darcy wanted nothing to do with her, she felt the pang of her loss of Darcy anew and sank deeper into a depressive spiral that brought her thoughts bouncing back and forth from Darcy to Bolivar. The loss of both were more than she could bear.

In her pajamas at noon one Saturday, she came across a sunflower seed shell near the trash can in the kitchen. Suddenly, she found herself in tears.

*How many times was I irritated with Bo for leaving sunflower seed shells behind him like Hansel and Gretel? Oh, God, what I would give to have him sitting here eating sunflower seeds, making some snarky comment about an article in the newspaper.*

She sank into her chair at the table. *When he talked to me, it was such an expanding experience. When I took in the way he had of telling me he loved me or his way of looking at the world, I cherished every word, every challenge to my mind and heart to open wider. I can't believe I'll never have that again.*

Slowly, she rose and went to the cupboard, took down a wine glass. She brought the glass to the cabinet that held wine bottles. Reaching down, she took out a bottle of red, uncorked it, and hesitated. Thoughts of Bo and Darcy overwhelmed her. *Just one glass today. It'll help me get through this.* She poured a large glassful of Malbec and took it to the table.

She heard a knock on the back door. Her pulse quickened. *Bolivar? Why would he knock? But who else would be knocking at the back door?*

"Hello? Anyone home?"

Jane opened the door to Louise, who stood on the back porch, suitcase beside her. "Surprise!" she said, holding her arms out. "I've come for a surprise visit." Receiving no response and noting Jane's dull eyes and disheveled state, she put her hands on her hips. "You sure are a ray of sunshine. What the hell's going on?"

"Bo's gone," Jane said in a lifeless voice. "He left me a month ago."

"Jesus Jehosaephat!" Louise picked up her suitcase and let herself inside.

Jane sat, elbow on the kitchen table, forehead in the palm of her hand. "Says he can't live with my bitterness anymore. And not only that. Bekah's back in touch with Darcy, but Darcy wants nothing to do with me."

"Oh man, that little shit."

She waved away Louise's judgment of her daughter. Recriminations that regularly tortured Jane twisted the knife in her heart. "Bekah broke through the lies she was fed, but maybe Darcy can't. Maybe she'll always believe I abandoned her."

"I knew it," Louise said. "I knew it. This little voice told me to come over. You said you would help me plan my wedding, but I don't need plans to elope! Something just said I needed to get over here."

Louise noted the full wine glass on the table, the uncorked bottle sitting next to it. "A little early, isn't it, sis?" She took the glass and raised her eyebrows skeptically at Jane, who shrugged.

"Oops!" Louise said, pouring it down the sink. She broke out in laughter that was too loud. "Dr. Reynalda warned me that drinking doesn't go with meds."

"What medicines?"

She opened and shut cupboard doors. "The ones we're gonna ask the doc to put you on. Now, you tell me all about that son-of-a-bitch Bo, that goddamn Darcy, the whole catastrophe. Where do you keep your tea bags?"

On Monday, Louise called the sub service, then the doctor's office. She stayed for a week, taking Jane to her appointment with the doctor and getting her started on anti-depressants. She held Jane's hand during her crying fits of despair and self-loathing in which she lamented giving up her girls. Louise made her tea, bought pizza for dinner, and made Jane eat it.

By the time Louise left for home, Jane was not entirely clear of the emotional morass, but she was putting distance between it and herself. As she hugged her sister good-bye, she felt confident returning to her classroom.

When she saw Bo in the hallway one afternoon, he looked gaunt and distracted. As for herself, she knew she was substantially better when her stomach merely plunged and she did not dissolve into tears.

After her daughters' reunion in Minnesota, Bekah kept Jane apprised of the relationship developing with her sister through daily online chats and occasional phone calls. Sometimes news from Bekah brought tears of joy, sometimes tears of frustration.

Bekah forwarded to Jane a particularly painful email Darcy had sent in response to an invitation to visit her in the Pacific Northwest when she and Ian stayed with his parents for the holidays.

*Dear Bekah,*

*I am writing because I've been thinking about your offer for me to go to Seattle and visit you when you're in town for the holidays.*

*I cannot visit you for one reason: I do not want to see Jane at all. Let me make myself perfectly clear: Jane is no longer my mother. I have a mother here that loves me and cares for me, and I love and care for her also. When Jane gave us up, she surrendered all her rights to me as her daughter and with that action, crushed any possibility of a future relationship with me. If I ever do change my mind, it will be on my terms and at my instigation.*

*Let me also make one other thing clear: although you are my sister and I love you very much, if you ever try to arrange any type of meeting to bring Jane back into my life, it will severely damage our relationship. For one, it will prove that I cannot trust you, and it will also show me that you do not respect my feelings or wishes.*

*Always, Darcy*

The heartache Jane suffered when she read Darcy's email was almost too much. It brought to the surface once again her deepest regret: she should never have given up the girls for adoption. *Have I lost Darcy forever?*

Bekah suffered for her mother. She had been hesitant about sharing the email. But more important was her need to let her mother know they could not rush things with Darcy. There was real danger, not only for Jane, but for Bekah as well, in trying to force a reconciliation.

"Damn, damn, damn! She won't even allow you to talk about me?" Jane fumed during one phone conversation with Bekah. "I don't know how much more I can stand."

"I don't know how you can have such patience," Bekah said.

"I've waited so long." Jane sighed. "God, I miss her!"

"Patience, Mom, patience," Bekah said. "I know it's not easy, but you know it's got to be at her pace."

"Yes . . . I know," Jane said. *She's so close! It's harder to wait now than during the years when they were so far away.*

Slowly, over many months, Darcy built her trust in the sister she loved. Bekah honored her sister's ban on discussions of Jane, until one particular phone conversation.

"Mom sent me a care package yesterday," said Bekah.

"You know I don't want to hear about Jane."

"She sent my all-time favorite candy. Remember when we were little and would've killed for a package of Pop Rocks?" She chuckled.

Darcy giggled. "Yeah."

"And she sent me two DVD's. *Footloose* and *Amadeus*. Foot loose, foot loose, kick off your Sunday shoes . . ."

Darcy joined in, a reflexive action of hundreds of duets sung in their childhood.

"We must've watched that movie a zillion times."

"Oh no, I'm sure I watched *Amadeus* two zillion times," Darcy said.

"I remember once when we came home from Dad's and you were upset about something. You had a headache and had been crying. Mom put on *Amadeus*, made some popcorn, and we all sat on the couch and watched your favorite movie. Twice, I think. She finally carried you up to bed."

Darcy was silent.

"Darcy?"

"Mm-hm."

Bekah said softly, "She loves you, sissy. Everything she's ever done was out of love for you and me."

"Like giving us up?"

"Think back to our lives before we went to live with Dad and Dolores."

Darcy was quiet a moment. "I remember one time she sat on the side of my bed when I'd come home after a weekend in Rathcreek. I confessed to her something I'd done that Dad thought was terrible. I don't even remember what it was, or how she responded. But I remember my feelings, and I remember saying to her that she was so much more understanding than Dad."

*Hallelujah! C'mon, Darcy. Come on!*

"You know Mom would never have done what she did without excruciating pain and, right or wrong, for what she thought was in our best interest. She's been waiting so long to hear from you, sissy."

In April, almost four years to the day after Bekah reunited with Jane, and ten years after Jane had lost Darcy, Jane received an email from Darcy.

*Hi Jane,*

*I know Bekah has been keeping you up to date with what we have been talking about, but I figured it was about time for me to stop being a big pansy and start talking to you.*

*Things are going all right for me. I've moved from Amherst to Austin, Texas, since I graduated from the university.*

*I don't really know where to start, what with
telling you what's going on in my life, since I would
basically have to start way far back, so I will let you
ask some questions and we can go from there.*

*Anyway, I guess I will let you go. Have a
good day.*

*Darcy*


Jane read the email again and again, and finally to
Louise over the phone.

"I'm ecstatic she wrote." She paused. "But she called
me Jane."

Louise brushed it aside. "Hey, she's *writing* to you!"

"Oh my God, yes! She *wrote* to me! She graduated and
moved to Austin. Isn't it funny she's in Austin? I didn't
know she was interested in living there. Why Texas?"

"Just be glad she didn't move back to Rathcreek,"
Louise said.

"Oh, man!" Jane shook her head. "Thanks for keeping
me on track."

"Yes, thank you, Jeezuz, for that," Louise said in an
ironic voice. "I'm sure you want to email her back right
away. So get to it, woman!"

"Thanks, sis."

"For what?"

"For being there to share my happiness with."

In times past, Jane would have relished sharing such
triumphs with Bolivar, but she couldn't bring herself to
do it.

Bo had left a message on her phone just after he'd moved
out to let her know where he was living. He stumbled a

bit, saying he was living with Elizabeth. "I'm living in her house anyway. There's nothing—nothing going on. You remember Elizabeth? She teaches history and lives close to the high school." Jane didn't know details, and it knocked the wind out of her.

Catching sight of Bo in the hallway at school made her stomach drop. She avoided him mostly, but it was not a large school—and they were in the same department. On the rare occasion they ran into each other in the teachers' lounge, whether anyone was around or not, each behaved as if the other were a ghost.

Today, however, she longed to share her news of Darcy with Bo. She picked up her cell phone, then put it down. She shook off the churning of her stomach and picked up the phone. It rang once, then went through to voice mail. She hung up.

It wasn't until she hung up that she realized she didn't simply want to share this important news. She wanted an excuse to talk to Bo after months apart. What she didn't know was whether he wanted to talk with her.

She made herself sit down at her computer. After reading Darcy's email one more time, her fingers flew over the keyboard.

> *Dear Darcy,*
>
> *It's wonderful to hear from you! I can imagine what an act of courage it was to decide to connect with me, not knowing how I might respond, not to mention the repercussions in Rathcreek. I've hoped for this day for a long, long time.*
>
> *It seems strange to have you call me Jane, although I understand, considering the idea you*

*may hold about a mother who doesn't love you, or she would never have let you go. The most important thing is this: when I read your name on an email in my inbox, my heart skips a beat. Several, actually. All I want to do is open my arms wide and hug you and tell you how much I love you, and will always love you, no matter what. I'm so sorry I hurt you, Darcy. I'd like to wish the past away, but I can't. So just know that I'm so happy you decided to contact me.*

*My love has always been there, even when you may have thought I took the easy way out. Believe me, my sweet daughter, there was nothing easy about the way I took.*

*Yes, Bekah's told me some of what you've talked about. Each detail about you she shared, I cherished. I know you're an ace ballet dancer and you graduated from the university with honors. You hold a BA in linguistics. You're smart and, from the high school photo Bekah showed me, beautiful. You're a little more conservative than your sister (no tattoos?). All this is just a rough sketch and doesn't really tell me who Darcy is at this moment of her life.*

*The easiest way to do this is by phone. Why don't you give me a call? (360) 555-1234. Let's talk tonight, okay? We have a lot of catching up to do.*

*Love, Mom*

There was no response from Darcy. Not that night or the next. Jane was beside herself, and it was all she could do to try to calm her fears. Finally, she sent a second email.

Hi Darcy,

*Okay, okay. I knew as soon as I sent my response that it was probably over the top, but I'd already pushed send! The prospect of your coming back into my life brought up more emotion than I could handle, I guess.*

*I'm sorry if it made you uncomfortable to be dealing with the fact that you're not just contacting 'Jane,' but Mom. Eeek! How could it not, when I'm talking to you as my daughter, which you were, for a dozen of the sweetest years of my life?*

*All I can say, Darcy, is that life is difficult, and our family has had more than its share of "difficult," considering what a blessed life we had before the break.*

*Anyway, I understand your reluctance to talk. It's scary. And for me, too. Look at how my exuberance has already screwed up this reunion. Shit! Give me another chance, okay? You can write or call, whatever you feel ready for. But please contact me.*

Love, Mom

Darcy answered her mother's email at 10:20 p.m. that evening. It was two short paragraphs.

*Thanks for the email. Bekah told me you were worried when I didn't call, so I am sorry for that, but I think I just need a little more time. Thanks for the last email with the extra understanding.*

*Anyway, I'm kinda down (from work) and just wanted to drop you a short note to let you know that I got your email, and I am happy that we have started talking again. I will try and write a better email a little later.*

*Darcy*

Jane was beside herself with joy. She wrote her back the following day.

*Hi Darcy,*

*So what are you up to? Do you feel like you're getting enough R & R over the weekend? What is it that's getting you down at work? Bekah told me you did have a tattoo! What is it and where? Tell me about your schooling. Did I get it right? Was it linguistics you majored in? What's your dream job? What career would make you really happy?*

*I'm not interested in going way back, as much as to know who you are now. I'm glad to know you feel that contacting me has been a good thing.*

*Love, Mom*

This message brought a longer email in response from Darcy. In it, she stated that even her Dad and Dolores did not receive such newsy emails from her, as it was not normally her way to write anything but quick updates.

Jane knew Darcy was more of an introvert compared to Bekah's extrovert personality. She was just beginning to know this adult daughter, and she told herself to respect Darcy for who she was and follow her rhythms and needs. It was not easy.

A couple of months after the first email, Darcy phoned Jane. Their phone call fell far short of the three-hour gab-fest of Bekah and Jane's first phone connection, but it was the beginning of a true link to her daughter. Jane asked question after question, Darcy answered them all, and they gently talked about the stop-and-go of their coming together.

"I don't know. I just needed time to feel safe," Darcy said.

"You feel safe now?"

"Pretty much." She added, "I know this must've been hard for you to wait until I was ready. I appreciate your understanding."

"You're more than welcome," Jane tried to say, but her voice failed. She cleared her throat and said it again in a thick voice. The wait was nothing to her now. This was the happily ever after she'd dreamed of for years.

Darcy said, "Well, it's been good to hear your voice again. But it's getting late. I'd better go."

Jane's insatiable heart ached to hold her just a little longer, to hear her voice, her laugh. But she said, "Yeah, I guess so."

Then, instead of hanging up, as if a thought just occurred to her, Darcy started off in a direction different from the small talk she'd felt safe engaging in. "You know, I was thinking about my childhood the other day, early childhood, when Bekah and I lived with you."

"Uh huh."

"And I realized that I had a really happy childhood. I just wanted you to know, Mom. I wanted you to know that *I* know."

A physical tightness took Jane's breath away. *She called me Mom! She remembers. She knows her childhood with me was happy.*

Of the many facets of their conversation, this revelation was one Jane would never forget.

But over the months that followed, Darcy put off meeting with her, saying she wasn't ready for the final step.

Yet, over time, her communications with Jane grew warmer. And the phone calls felt safer as Jane gently probed without judgment and Darcy felt safe to answer questions as she would a trusted friend. Both seemed relieved to be free to tease and laugh, to confess fears and reassure.

A few months later, on Christmas Eve, they finally met on what Darcy considered safe ground in Bekah and Ian's sparsely furnished apartment in Minneapolis. Bekah opened the door to her sister's knock, hugged her quickly, then stood aside. When Darcy first saw her mother, she hung back shyly, standing in the doorway.

"Oh my God. Look at you!" Jane cried. She walked forward and threw her arms around Darcy. She was so overjoyed at seeing her daughter for the first time in a decade, hers was a love not to be withstood, even by Darcy, who hesitated, then melted into her mother's embrace.

"I've waited so long for this!" Jane said, eyes filled with tears.

"Me, too, Mom," said Darcy in a choked voice.

When Darcy called her Mom, a thrill ran through Jane.

The girls were sad to hear Bolivar would not be joining them, but was spending Christmas with Simon on the ski slopes. Jane chided herself for not telling the girls the truth about Bo, for being such a coward. But she could not bear the thought of marring the first Christmas in years with her daughters.

In the rosy glow of Christmas tree lights early Christmas morning, Jane sipped her coffee. The tree was piled high with gaily wrapped gifts. She had brought suitcases packed with presents, making up for the years she had not been allowed to send anything to her daughters.

Both girls loved their gifts, but Darcy was especially touched by a story Jane had found that little Darcy had written in large, round letters, as a ten-year-old who was in love with books. When Darcy read it aloud, she had Bekah in stitches at her attempt at being literary. Darcy read more, until she and her sister were howling. In the small living room taken over by the tree and its glowing lights and by her family reunited, Jane joined in the laughter. The voltage of her love of her daughters in this moment powered her capacity to feel content.

Darcy and Bekah were delighted with Jane's gift of two photo albums she had put together of pictures of each of them when they were little. Funny pictures, silly ones, some warm and loving with arms around their mother's neck that Uncle Bob and Aunt Ruth had taken. A few were with Bob and Ruth and Bo and Simon. Jane looked on from a distance as they showed each other the photos, recounted happier times.

After Darcy opened the box that contained an Xbox, she came over and held out her arms to Jane. "These tears are not because I loved the Xbox so much—which, yes, I do—but because Christmas for years has been strictly about the birth of Jesus and not about gifts. Nothing like my memories of Christmases we shared for so many years as a time to celebrate family."

Jane gathered her daughter into her arms. Her eyes filled with tears and it was hard to breathe. Darcy's hug incapacitated her, took away any language her mind might have had to name how she felt. She was all feeling, and she only knew she wanted to remember this moment forever. She smelled Darcy's sweet perfume, felt the thick sweater over her daughter's slender shoulders.

Christmas had always been the one time of the year Jane felt she could spoil the girls, and a little over-indulgence was a treat for her as well as for them. She had gone to great lengths to be sure this Christmas holiday had the same feel as it had so many years ago.

Later that day, the three women were in Bekah's kitchen chopping onions and celery for the dressing that would go into the turkey, laughing at stinging eyes and tears.

Darcy put down the chef's knife. "Where's your ski gear?" she asked Bekah.

"What? Why?"

"Just show me." Darcy pulled her sister by two fingers out of the kitchen.

When they came back, Darcy was wearing ski goggles and Bekah trailed behind her giggling.

Darcy gave her mom a thumbs up. "See? My college education was worth every penny!"

Jane chuckled. Darcy, chopping, so ridiculous, her dark eyes behind the rosy visor of the goggles.

"So—" Jane hesitated. "I'm sure your education cost plenty. Do you have any student loans I can help with?"

"Nah."

"Nah?" Jane asked, incredulous. Logan certainly must not have wanted his daughter to go to a university, where she could be swayed by heathens. Had he paid for it?

"Darcy was in ROTC when she was in high school, since Dad said he wouldn't contribute to our education," Bekah said. "That's how you did it, isn't it?"

Darcy nodded. "I'm signed up for four years with the Army now that I'm finished, as an officer, and my under grad education is paid for."

The news felt like an arrow to Jane's heart. "You—you're in the Army?"

"Yup," Darcy said. "A lieutenant."

Jane tried to breathe. Her wounded heart seemed to bang against her ribs. *Darcy looks so proud of herself, as if the possibility of trading her life for no student loan debt is a good deal.* "So that means you could be sent to Afghanistan?"

"Don't worry, Mom," Darcy said. "It's not a combat position. I'd be a lieutenant in intelligence, well protected, away from the action."

The only thing Jane could think of was IED's. She heard reports on the morning news about roadside bombs, improvised explosive devices, blowing up soldiers who were *away from the action.*

Darcy put her hand on Jane's arm. "Really, Mom. I'll probably pull a desk gig back here in the States or in Germany."

*Oh my God,* Jane thought, and gave Darcy a weak smile. *I can't stand it. And, dammit, I can't say anything. I can't add to the anxiety Darcy's got to be feeling about being shipped off*

*overseas to a war zone. Keep her safe. Keep her safe. Don't
take her from me now.*

Jane glanced around the room, trying to hold onto
this reality, her daughter's apartment, the girls preparing
dinner, snow coming down outside these windows. They
were all safe in Minneapolis and she was having Christmas
with her daughters, both daughters, at long last.

The kitchen was small and painted off-white, as with
most apartments, but Jane noted it was spotless, with dishes
still drying in the rack on the counter. She took a frayed
towel from the railing on the oven door and finished drying
the dishes and putting them away in the cupboard. Christmas music played on a CD player on the kitchen table. The
scent of pumpkin pie made the room smell like Christmas.

"Hey, guess what?" Bekah said. "Ian's got the Minneapolis store up and running, so he's been transferred again.
We're moving to Santa Cruz, California, in a month."

"But you'll miss the sub-zero Minneapolis winters!"
Darcy laughed and gave her sister a high five.

"Wow! Congratulations to Ian," Jane said. "Closer to
Washington. You'll be easier to visit."

At dinner, the conversation meandered peacefully
until Jane asked, "So, now that you and Darcy are back
together, are you back in touch with Logan and Dolores,
Bekah?" Immediately, she regretted bringing it up.

"No." Bekah wrinkled her nose.

"I was telling her it might be time to extend the olive
branch," Ian said in his easy-going way.

"And I said I'm not ready to extend even a leaf," said
Bekah, taking a sip of wine.

The sound of forks and knives scraped dinner plates,
punctuated by Xia, Bekah's Siamese cat, who jumped up

on the kitchen counter. Ian got up from the table and shooed her down.

"I'm not ready to forgive them for coming between Darcy and me. Not to mention all the damage they caused with their freakin' faith in the first place."

Darcy kept her eyes on her plate.

"All the times they tried to contact me, they never said a damn thing about assuming one bit of responsibility for breaking apart this family, for making us so hateful. For making our mom give us up." Bekah picked up her wine glass and finished off the last swallow before pouring another glassful. "They owe us an apology and you an apology," she said to Jane. "Darcy and I have talked about it, and even if she won't say it, she can see what they did. She's seen the light."

Jane felt like a pinball, careening from one shocker to the next. *They* both *know the truth.* In her heart, there was an ache, that her daughters should ever have to go through such pain.

She took in the tension around the table. She studied her fiery daughter. The anguish she read in her daughter's eyes sickened her. The fallout was still a part of her. She looked at Darcy, who moved food around her plate, finally seeing reality, but stricken, having to deal plainly with her parents' actions.

Jane took a deep breath. "I don't know if they will ever be able to take responsibility. I've talked with them. My impression is they weren't—ah—" she glanced at Darcy, "exactly based in this reality." She looked at Bekah, head down and arms crossed. She said softly, "But I do know this: forgiving doesn't mean you have to trust them; it's for you, not them. Forgiving is simply a means for the truth of what you went through to escape, besides crawling out the hole it's eaten in your belly."

# 11

On their last day in Minneapolis, Bekah drove Darcy and Jane to the airport. As Bekah roamed through the radio channels, they heard church music.

Jane took in the slight movement of her daughters' heads, their looks to each other. They were communicating as twins, the way they always had, without saying a word.

"It took a while before the sound of church music didn't make me feel anxious," Jane said.

Bekah said, "I'm not anxious. I'm pissed."

"Me, too," Darcy said.

"Okay. I understand." Jane was quiet a moment, looking out the window as the town in its mantle of white moved past them. The grandeur and vastness of nature filled her with reverence.

"It's always been the mystery that moves us." Jane didn't wait for an answer, but followed the thread of her thoughts as they fell into place. "Isn't it funny that once you find out no one has the ultimate answer about God, you're set free to be awestruck by your contemplation of this big, beautiful world and the mystery of our existence. Think of it, religions corral us into a narrow box of beliefs fed to us by all these yahoos behind their pulpits. They tell us if we don't believe what we've been fed, if we consort with others who aren't buying what we've been fed, we'll be led astray and burn forever. Getting free means we can enjoy peaceful interactions with anyone—whether they share our beliefs or not. Which is why I describe myself as a humanist. People. It's all about here and now. My God, I'm glad you broke free. I love you both so much."

"Wow, that was pretty good, Mom," Bekah said. Darcy turned to the back seat and gave her mother a smile.

"What was the name of that book you were telling me about—something delusional?" Jane asked.

Darcy laughed. "*The God Delusion* by Richard Dawkins."

"I'll have to pick up a copy. Wish I'd had it a long time ago."

"It's a game changer," Darcy said.

Back home after the winter break, Jane returned to her classroom. It was a struggle getting her students into their routine after the holidays, but Jane was quick on her feet and wily in her approach to herding teens who flaunted their resistance to learning. One tactic was sharing her enthusiasm for literature. She wasn't shy about donning a blonde Pollyanna-type wig to teach about the optimism inherent in Transcendentalism, or wearing a purple sweatshirt with a red hat and bright yellow and black striped stockings to pull them into a poem about a woman who chose to wear purple.

"Your brain is like a muscle," she told her students. "You have to use it. And the more you use it, the bigger it gets." She leaned down to a dark haired student in the front row who was flexing his muscles. "You don't want to stay a little brain after all your friends have buffed up and moved on to solving the world's problems, do you?"

He looked up at Jane, face wreathed with a smirk. "No, I don't want to stay little. I want to run for president some-day, where size matters."

Jane lost control of her class. When it was quiet again and she'd gotten her own laughter under control, she said, "Okay, okay. Yes, we've studied double entendres—and Will's is a pretty good one. Look for a question on defining that term on Friday's quiz."

At the end of the school day, Jane was filled with optimism and love: of her daughters and her students. Bolivar came to mind. The depth of despair she felt at the loss of his love surfaced and threatened to take her under. She recalled their early years and the wonder of their love, the way they were drawn to each other, the feeling that their relationship was somewhere between a beloved recurring dream and a well-known story of true love. She had always found it miraculous that they so perfectly filled each other's needs for intimacy and con-nection. Not to mention the way her loins longed for him in a way that used to bring her to her knees. Bolivar's sweet succulent kisses. Gone forever?

"This is ridiculous," she said aloud. *I don't care if Bo turns me down and I'm humiliated. I'm not giving up on us until I confront him and fight for us. If there's one thing I'm sure of, it's that love is worth fighting for. Hell, Shakespeare says it's worth dying for.*

Jane shoved the remainder of ungraded papers into her briefcase, turned off the lights, and locked the door behind her. She walked down the hallway and knocked on a classroom door.

Bo sat before a stack of papers that threatened to topple, his pen scribbling something on the one in the center of his desk.

He looked up. "Jane! How are you?" His face lit up like a boy who had unexpectedly thrown a ring around a bottle neck at the fair. Then worry crept in to muddle the look. His face grew serious and he put down his pen.

"I'm fine. How are you?"

"Fine—for having just collected a shit-load of papers to grade. You'd think after Christmas break these guys would know how to write a five-paragraph paper, wouldn't you?"

"Naw, that doesn't happen until June, when you're waving good-bye. Then you get a whole new batch in the fall who don't know a five-paragraph paper from a text message, and you start all over again."

The tension in his face relaxed into a smile. "What can I do for you?"

She stood there, feeling suddenly impulsive, stupidly optimistic. But her yearning for Bo outweighed the discomfort of her insecurity.

"I'd like to invite you over for a celebratory dinner."

He pursed his lips and said, mocking, "You getting married?"

*Always over the top*, she thought, the comfortable back-and-forth of their humor bolstering her. "Nope. I've reconnected with Darcy. I want to celebrate with you, since you, more than anyone, know what it means to me."

He gave her a brilliant smile and looked as if he would hug her. "Jane, that's great. Fantastic."

She smiled, nodded. "That is, if Elizabeth can spare you as a dinner partner for the night."

"Look, Jane, I'm just renting a basement apartment—which is a toilet that doesn't flush right and a bed that my feet hang over. There was never anything between us." He reached out and took her hand. "I'd love to come over." He hesitated, then, as if throwing his heart at her feet, "I've missed you."

"I've missed you, too."

That evening, she had butterflies in her stomach when she answered the door.

At dinner, they ate by candle light, enjoyed the wine Bo brought, and laughed like old times. They talked about news old and new, about Jane being in touch with Darcy. Bo took her hand and toasted Darcy "finally seeing the light."

And when Jane shared her student's comment that day, Bo chuckled and said, "I thought I taught you everything I knew about getting students engaged in their learning, but you got me beat by miles."

She touched his cheek softly with the back of her hand. "Oh, I don't know about that. You taught me plenty from the time I was your student. I took careful notes about what to do when all hell breaks loose when some genius says something that destroys the decorum of the classroom."

The phone rang, the ringtone indicating one of her daughters was calling.

"It's Bekah or Darcy."

Bo nodded and she got up to retrieve her cell phone.

"Hi, Mom. Just calling to let you know we're getting ready to shove off and head to California."

"Wow! The time went fast! Are you excited?"

"Yeah. Also freaked out. Too much to do in too little time."

"I can imagine. Didn't you say you'd be driving? When do you expect to arrive?"

Bekah was silent a moment, then said. "Yeah, that's what I wanted to talk to you about."

Jane walked into the dining room and mouthed *Bekah* to Bolivar.

"You know the car we drove from Washington to Minnesota, the one you and Bo cosigned for?"

"Yes."

"Well, it's a piece of crap. Got all kinds of mechanical problems. We've been looking into having it fixed, but it's really not worth it for how much it'll cost us."

"So how are you going to drive to California?"

"We bought a new car. Well, a used car. It's beautiful and it runs perfect. It'll get us across the country and we won't have to worry about repairs. Hopefully, at least for a while."

Jane was silent a moment. "Have you sold the other car?" Worry wormed its way through her brain and she hoped that Bekah and Ian would not be struggling under the weight of two car payments.

"Well, that's just it. We can't sell it, because it's not running. In fact, we've been taking the bus to work, and it's been parked in front of a friend's place for a couple months now."

"So what are you going to do?"

Bekah cleared her throat. "We're going to leave it and hopefully, our friend can sell it for scrap or something that will at least get it cleared out from the street in front of his apartment. We told him he could keep whatever he got for it for his trouble."

With a growing sense of dread, Jane asked, "And so you have how many more payments to make on it?"

"Only about three months." She hesitated. "But we've got to just let it go. We can't afford to make two car payments."

"But it will affect your credit rating, honey—and ours, since we cosigned for your loan." She glanced at Bo and saw the worry etched in his forehead.

Bekah was silent.

Bo poured himself another glass of wine and watched Jane.

"Honey, you can't just let it go. You signed a contract. We signed it guaranteeing that you would pay off this car."

"I know, Mom, but—" She sounded as though she knew she sounded lame even to herself. "With the moving expenses and buying another car to make sure we make it across the country—we really can't afford it."

"Just so I'm clear on this, you're not going to pay off this loan Bo and I cosigned?"

Bekah was silent again, then said softly, "Sorry, Mom."

"Okay, I get it. You can choose to take the easy way out, but you know, there's always consequences to our actions."

In Bekah's silence, she knew the discussion was over. There was nothing left for her daughter to say.

Jane hung up and filled in Bolivar.

"What can they be thinking?" he said. "Doesn't she know what she's doing to her credit rating? To ours?"

"I don't think she can see any way around it. It's not like they were given time by Zumiez to save up for the move. She told me Ian was given notice to move when I went out there at Christmas to meet Darcy."

Bo nodded.

"Bekah announced that they were moving and had about a month's notice. I didn't realize they were already using public transportation. Driving across the country to California is a whole different story."

"So." Bo swirled the wine in his glass. The light caught the red, a blush splashing its way around the glass.

The old fear welled up in Jane. They were bickering again about Bekah. Even from afar, her daughter was contributing to strife between them.

"Well, first, I'm sorry Bekah's not being responsible," Jane said.

One thing was sure: the hit she would take with car payments during the next three months would require sacrifice—the kind of sacrifice her daughter and Ian, who loved tattoos as much as Bekah, were not willing to make.

"I don't think there's any choice but to pay the last three payments, to keep our credit rating clean. Don't you think?"

"Yup, we're pretty much screwed if we don't," Bo said. "Lesson learned, I guess. And Bekah has to learn that she can have tattoos or money in the bank for emergencies, but not both." He drank the remaining wine in his glass, pushed back from the table, and headed to the door.

Jane said after him, "It's not like there's anything I could've done."

Bo plodded forward, wrapping a scarf around his neck. He raised his hand over his head in a back-handed wave before he closed the door behind him.

Jane pounded the table with her fist.

⁂

Shortly after Bekah and Ian's move to Santa Cruz, her sister received orders for Afghanistan.

Darcy was part of a nine-month deployment to Afghanistan of the 1st Calvary Division's 4th Brigade Combat Team. It would be the first time a brigade-level unit from the division, nearly 1,400 soldiers who were part of the Long Knife Brigade and its subordinate battalions, was deployed to Afghanistan. They were expected to leave Fort Hood within the month.

"A month?" Jane said into the phone, her fingertips to her forehead.

"I didn't want to worry you," Darcy replied. "Now don't you give me a hard time. Bekah already chewed me out for being *in* the Army rather than being a protester against the war, like she is."

"But I thought our troops were already pulled out."

"Yes, but some still provide support," Darcy said. "My brigade will field about 16 security force assistance advisory teams to advise and assist the Afghan army and police forces. Air Force warplanes and drones are going to be available, too."

Jane said quietly, "So you knew about being shipped out a year ago when you moved to Texas?"

"I've known it for a long time. Just didn't want to cause undue stress by being out there about it, since reconnecting to you and Bekah was stressful enough."

Jane tried to calm herself, but her heart raced. The hysterical voice inside was out of control, pointing out that it would be just like fate, in a supreme act of irony to take Darcy from her, now that they had finally reconnected. She thought about how her heart skipped, as if to music, whenever she heard her daughter's voice when she picked up the phone. How much she loved to send Darcy emails and read the ones she sent back. And now Darcy would be in Afghanistan? Being shot at? Even if she was not directly involved in combat, she would be dodging IED's on the road into and out of that country. It was almost more than Jane could bear.

"Is there time for me to fly down and visit before you go?"

"I don't think so. It would just make it harder for me. So you, Dad and Dolores, and Bekah all want to come down—that's just too much. I'll write. Promise."

Jane knew it was too much for her sensitive daughter. Darcy needed to focus on her mission, without the distractions of family members who would only cause her fears to grow larger.

"Goodnight Saigon" came to mind. The lyrics always brought her to the verge of tears, especially when she heard war stories on the radio news of the young men and women in Iraq and Afghanistan. It was a different war than the song referred to, but the horror of war, the loss of life, the life-long injuries were the same.

And now her daughter was promising she'd write.

"I understand. I love you, Darcy."

"I love you, too, Mom."

# 12

Logan Churlick awoke from a dream. He was breathing heavily and his eyes, barely opened slits, gave him a feel for his surroundings. He took a calming breath, smelling the room, and tried to relax. He was powerfully aroused. The dream would not leave him.

The clock read 4:32 a.m. Curled up in bed under thick covers, he enjoyed the warmth and the residual fullness from the dream's stimulation.

*Jane*, he thought, and quietly turned toward the wall. A murky early morning light flooded into the room through the lace curtains. He listened and heard the steady breathing of Dolores next to him.

The dream had been so vivid, he was still under its spell. He made himself to go back to the dream, to Jane. He willed her back. He spotted her, standing with her back to him. He walked slowly to her, creating the scene from the beginning, to taste the fullness of it.

Fate had handed her to him as her marriage was falling apart so he could counsel her. As her minister, he stood above her in the coolness of his dimly-lit office.

"I loved you like a father since you were a little girl. I always thought of you as my special one." His voice caught, and it surprised him how the words unlocked an ache, an image of a kind-hearted little girl who was loved by everyone and who everyone loved; his Janey, his delight, skinny legs, arms around his neck, exuberant, high-pitched giggle, teeth too big for her small face. The teeth now graced a smooth-skinned woman sitting before him. Hope tormented him and he longed for her. "I always loved you, Janey. I thought you loved me, too."

"I do," she cried. "You know I do, Reverend Churlick."

Joy flooded through his veins like a burning intoxicant. She loved him. He had known it, and now she said it for the first time. He would remember the moment forever. He stared at Jane, the anguish he read in her face exquisite.

If he had to admit it, he was addicted to her magnificent, burgeoning strength that came from two months of her counseling sessions with him. He craved her beauty, her intelligence, and more than anything craved her strength submitting to his authority.

Logan's eyes were closed. Rousing himself from his lethargic state, he pictured her smiling up at him. He stroked himself gently.

Her smile, radiant, holding nothing back, chased by the glimmering laugh. The wry hazel eyes, incredibly alive eyes, so unlike Dolores' faded blues, bleak with fear, empty.

"I want your love!" Jane said, and looked away, suddenly bashful. He took her hands and his mind encouraged her to say more.

"I've always wanted your love," she went on, "but there's Bolivar and you have Dolores."

"She doesn't mean anything whatsoever to me!" He hissed. He gazed into the sparkling eyes, saw her openness and goodness. "And we have our children to think about, my dear. They're a gift from God. And you know they need both parents." His voice was rich and he saw that it filled her with confidence to say the thoughts she had locked away.

Jane murmured, "They do. I know you're right. You've always been right." The silence. His touch.

"Say it, Janey. Say what's going on in your mind. I have to know."

She hesitated, then speaking softly, her warm voice filled his ear. "My love for you is so deep, Logan. Inexpressible. After all these years, absolutely inexpressible." She pulled back and her look was so intimate, so starkly yearning.

Images of the two of them in his study 20 years ago. Jane on the leather couch, the stifling heat outside bearing in on the room.

He nodded, patting her arm. "How can a woman commit her heart and will to such a big thing as obeyin' God when she can't even obey a man? That's your burden, Janey. Mine is to know how God would have me command you." He leaned forward, body taut. "Do you trust me? To lead you in God's way?"

"Yes."

He smiled, tearful, and blinked rapidly, bird-like. He could see his gaze held her: intense, compelling, an expression more ancient than a bird's. Reptilian.

He fell to his knees, took her hand and pulled her down to the carpet where they both knelt. A cool, musty breeze from the straining air conditioner moved around them. He stroked her hair with a trembling hand. He licked dry lips. A shiver ran through him.

"Thank you, heavenly Father. That's right. Let me hold you a minute, Janey. Jesus loves you. An' I've loved you so long. All for this moment."

He could see that she wanted him fiercely, like an animal with its nostrils flared, catching a scent that brought juices to her mouth. Tears welled in her eyes and she moved closer, pressing into him. He could feel her against him and it drove him wild with desire to hold her so she would never get away. He wanted to open his mouth and devour her in an instant, but he knew she needed to want him. She had to want him as much as he wanted her.

"Janey?" Tentatively, he tightened his embrace.

For a long moment, she was perfectly still. He gazed down at her, holding her tight, fear of her refusal in every breath he took. Then suddenly she melted into him, yielding as if from the powerful potion of words he injected her with.

"My God, my God," he murmured, and stared at her as if she were something sacred. "Such a woman, a gift from God. You're everything to me, Janey. Everything."

Her smile radiated happiness. She gave herself completely to the way he needed her. She lifted her face to him. Hungrily, he kissed her mouth, her neck, the curve of her breast, leaning her onto the couch. His grazing mouth rained relentlessly over her until her mouth obeyed. He caressed her breasts gently, worshipfully.

He murmured a soft moan, stroking surely as he had so many nights over the years. Her desire of him raised his own fury of desire to an unknown plane, one that lifted him from the misery of his defeated life to the rapture of possessing the only thing he had ever wanted. Jane Crownheart Bernard was once again totally his.

He turned his head to stifle the sound and mouthed into his pillow during the crescendo of his orgasmic spasm, "Ja-a-a-a-ne!"

On the other side of the bed, Dolores, who earlier had taken her nightly sleeping pill and chased it down with a large glass of wine, as was most nights her habit, had her back to him. Her frame moved slightly from the activity taking place a short ways from her. Dolores lifted her heavy eyelids.

At breakfast, Dolores moved about, sluggish but dogged, frying eggs, slathering butter on toast, fixing her husband's coffee. Finally, when Logan was provided for, she sat down heavily at the table and stared into her black coffee.

Logan looked up. "What?"

"Nothing."

The strident voices of Fox news radio in the background jangled his nerves and his wife's sulking irritated him.

He sighed and glanced at his watch, noting that it was almost time to leave for the church. The irritation caused by Dolores slipped away. Logan remained caught up in the echoes of his still vibrant emotions. He felt the glow of having possessed Jane, the dream gleaming like gold in the shabby kitchen.

"It's just that all these years we've been together, raising our daughters, and I feel like you never gave up your fantasy of having that bitch rather than me."

Logan's cup stopped in mid-air. He set it down. "You are really a piece of work. So insecure. I don't have to listen to this crap." He got up from the table and took his jacket from the back of his chair.

"When's the last time you made love to me?" Dolores cried, hand clutching her bathrobe.

"What are you talking about?" He slipped his jacket on and turned to face her, squaring off.

"You never make love to me. You haven't made love to me in six months, a year, I don't know how long."

Logan frowned. "Look at yourself! You're a slovenly cow. Only time you get gussied up is for church. And you pester me all the time. What makes you think I'd ever want you like that?"

Dolores ran a hand over her hair. "That's not true. I keep myself up. Get my hair colored, my nails done. I lost the weight. Still, you don't want me." She looked up at him, her words a challenge. "You only want your dream slut."

The hair on the back of Logan's neck rose. *She knows.* And the thought ignited a fury in him. "You're the slut!" he screamed. "If it weren't for your slutty past, we could've had kids of our own."

He looked wildly around the kitchen. "You're the reason everything's turned to shit. You're the one who sent all those letters to the girls, got them so worked up about Jane that she had no choice but to cut all of us out of her life. And now look. She's got them back. Both of 'em. And we're out in the cold. You don't give a shit about losing Bekah and Darcy. You just want to get screwed." He came over and grasped Dolores' quivering chin.

She screamed in pain, "Stop it!" wrenched her jaw away, and stood up.

They breathed deeply, facing each other. Mournful music played on the radio, now that the news program had finished.

"I don't know why I ever loved you," she said. "But I don't anymore. I know this, you've made my life a waste. I loved your bastard kids because you needed me to make our lives picture perfect. Now that they're gone, you blame me, treat me like dirt. You're scum."

Logan's head jerked back.

"That's right," she said. "Nobody sees it but me. Everybody thinks you're this wonderful man of God. But you're evil. Maybe it's time somebody other than me knew just how evil you are." A lock of perfectly dyed hair fell over her forehead and she brushed it aside.

Logan had never feared his wife. She had always seemed so powerless. He had made sure she didn't get any ideas that would raise her up. The fear of such an insurrection by someone so powerless unnerved him. It reminded him of the time as a seventeen-year-old he had tried to raise up against his father.

Not only was it a fruitless revolt, but he had never been able to shake the life-long fear from the incident. His father stood for iron-fisted house rules at a time young Logan had a driving need for attention from a certain girl he had a crush on. He was told in no uncertain terms to be home directly after the school football game. But Logan had seen Donna at the game that evening and decided to come home to get his father's approval to go to the dance afterward.

"No. You're not going to any dance," his father said, looking up from the Bible in his lap. "Playground of the devil."

"But Dad, there's this girl I like and I just want to—"

"I said *no!*" He slammed the Bible shut and rose from his chair. "A girl, you say? You can see her at church. She does go to church, doesn't she?"

Logan squirmed, looked down at his shoes.

"Well, I'll be. She's a heathen?" He said derisively, "What are you thinking?"

The son locked eyes with his father, feeling a new power surge through him, a strength he did not know he possessed, hormone-driven. For the first time, he saw his father through the heat of righteous indignation, fueled by a hatred of such indifference to his needs. He clenched his fists. "I don't like any of the girls at church. I like Donna. You can't keep me from seeing her."

Logan was as tall as his father but didn't have the bulk. And for someone with bulk, his father moved fast. Before Logan knew what was happening, he was pinned to the wall.

His father was breathing hard. "Now you listen to me." Bunches of Logan's shirt were in his fists. "Not only are you forbidden from going to the dance, but you are forbidden from going to any more football games, dances, anything after three o'clock when you should be home from school."

Logan wailed. "That's not fair! What about debate club? I didn't do anything. I came home to get permission."

He looked at Logan with narrowed eyes. "You came home to put one over on me."

"You're wrong," Logan said and struggled to break free.

Before he could say more, his father's fist came back and crashed into his nose. Blood squirted from the nose and drops splashed down Logan's face, dripped down his shirt and onto the floor. His hands flew to his nose and he howled in pain.

"You gonna question my authority?" his father said, unbuckling his belt. He slid it out of belt loops.

"No, Dad, I—"

The belt came down hard enough that the spot would become a welt on his raised hand. He yowled in pain, lost his footing and fell to the floor. He raised his arms against his father. Again and again, his father brought down the belt, slashing Logan's head, his arms, whatever wasn't protected by his hands.

*Mom*, he thought, wishing she were still alive. But his mother had died several years ago after being stung to death by a hive of hornets she had unwittingly disturbed while working in the garden they had in Texas.

Crying and shrieking at the hideous pain, he tried to scoot away, tried to get up, and slipped in the slick blood that now ran freely from his nose. His father was like a rabid animal at the mercy of a rage that twisted his ability to reason.

The beating went on, until Logan thought his father would beat him unconscious. The urgency of such a frightful thought gave him new strength, and he managed to get to his feet. He ran to the fireplace and grabbed the poker. He snarled, "One more time, and I swear, I'll kill you."

Breathing hard, his father stopped. He studied his son as he fed the belt through the loops of his pants. "You're not killin' anyone. You're a girl. Don't you ever challenge me again, or I swear this will seem like a tea party." He turned and walked toward the bedroom. "An' clean this mess up."

Now Logan considered whether Dolores's threat of defaming him was possible. It was. And ultimately, it would ruin the vague idea he had of reclaiming his daughters, and possibly recapturing Jane's heart, if Darcy's innocent revelation of Jane visiting her alone at Christmas was true. He was sure there was something to it that Jane wasn't revealing to Darcy. He and Dolores must be the united front they had always been.

He lowered his chin. "Dolores. Darlin'. You're a bundle of emotions." He walked slowly toward her and she slowly backed up. "But who do you think parishioners are gonna believe. You or me?"

She was silent.

"You can get ideas in that pretty little head of yours and they just don't make any sense. I didn't know you wanted more lovin'. I would of been more interested if you'd a told me, rather than beating around the bush."

The hope in Dolores' face lifted her lips into a reluctant smile. She didn't want to believe, but couldn't help believing.

"That's right," Logan said, smiling. "You get the wine chilled before I come home tonight, and we'll see what happens."

# 13

Jane paced the kitchen, then sat down on a chair. She stared at her phone for a couple of minutes, took a deep breath, and clicked on a number to dial.

"Hi. It's me."

"Hello." Bo's voice was rich and strong.

Her stomach fluttered. "Um. Listen—I've been thinking that we need to talk."

"Fire away. By the way, what's the word on our credit rating?""

"Yeah. I know. You've got every right to be snide. I've been making payments the past couple months. One more month and I'm done."

Bo's voice softened. "Why didn't you tell me? I would've chipped in."

"You left in such a—I mean it seemed things between us had broken down and—"

"I was pissed, I'll admit it. In fact, I was acting like I used to accuse you of. Like no feelings in the world mattered but mine. But if you'd called me, I wouldn't have left you holding the bag by yourself. We've got kids, and they make us crazy sometimes, but they won't break us apart—unless we let them. Hell, you can't imagine what Simon's up to these days."

Jane closed her eyes. "Oh, Bo. You don't know what a relief it is to hear you say that. I really need to talk to you. I mean I want to hear all about Simon. But there's news about Darcy."

"Is she okay?"

"Yes, so far. I'll tell you all about it when we meet."

"Huh. That's a hook if I ever heard one. So how 'bout tonight? Dinner?"

"Dinner tonight sounds great. But I've been thinking and it's more than dinner I need. I think it's time we took a chance and got to know one another again." Jane held her breath.

"You mean that in the biblical sense?"

He always knew how to puncture her calm. A giggle escaped.

"I mean, I'm feelin' lucky as a rabbit who's got all four feet."

"Let's get our Friday started, then, Roger," she said.

The evening was a blending of hearts and minds, sitting close together on the red couch talking deep into the night. First, Jane asked about the nature of Bo's relationship with Elizabeth. He laughed, then seeing her face, stopped, took her hand.

"It's funny to me, because there's absolutely no way. But let me put it this way: if the situation were reversed, I'd want to know. Fact is, I probably would've knocked the block off of any man who took you into a basement apartment. I know how it looks. But Jane, I give you my word, there's never been anything between us. Not one meal shared. When I left you, I wanted solitude to sort things out, not a woman. And I will tell you this is true: there isn't a woman alive who can make my heart sing the way you do."

A flutter of contentment winged its way through Jane. She leaned over and Bo took her in his arms to kiss, to certify that what he said was true.

The wine helped each of them let go of their pride, their defensiveness. Bo's talk of Simon was surprising in its candor, as if he didn't feel the need to one-up Jane about Simon's virtues compared to her girls' faults. Simon had his issues with grades at the university, with the women he dated, with having his head screwed on right, as was the case with most twenty-somethings.

Jane offered solace, then broached her concern that Bekah's behavior seemed to always be an obstacle to peace in their relationship. She brought up Darcy's imminent military duty, saying she couldn't stand the thought of losing her just when she'd gotten her daughter back into her life. Bo comforted Jane while she cried and she nuzzled him, making wet promises.

Head on his chest, Jane sniffed, and said thickly, "My girls mean everything to me, you know that. At the same time, I need to tell you that you're the center of my existence."

He took her teary face in his hands. "I know I'm home. You're home to me, Jane. I'm never going to leave again."

The kiss was a covenant, long and luxurious. She could not remember the last time they had kissed like that. Her heart knew things were new between them.

Bo took her hand and they stood, he enveloping her in his embrace. She raised her face to him, and they kissed again, both of them initiating the passionate connectedness. Arm in arm, they walked upstairs to the bedroom.

The next day, Jane yawned, raised her arms above her head, and pointed her toes, stretching luxuriously in bed.

She opened her eyes to find Bo staring at her. He smiled his disarming smile, the one that filled her with love and longing. She reached over and caressed his face.

"Morning, love," she said in a scratchy voice.

"Morning. I've been watching you breathe. So soft. You barely stir the air. You breathe in and out, mostly quietly, but sometimes you talk a little in your sleep." He gently stroked her arm, found his way to her waist, her hip, feeling the warm fullness of her. "God, I love you. I've missed you."

"Oh, Bo, I've missed you so much. I'm so sorry . . ."

Bolivar shushed her and reached for her hand. "I'm sorry, Jane. Sorry for both of us and what we had to go through. Sorry I wasn't by your side. I'm glad to be by your side now. And I always will be."

❧

*August 10*

*Dear Mom,*

*Okay, I never doubted your judgment in books. I mean, all the way back to my earliest memories, I remember you choosing good books for me. But I REALLY liked The Thornbirds that you sent in my last care package. If you have any other recommendations, please send!*

It's getting hot here. Yesterday it was 120 degrees. And the water is not very good quality. Doesn't matter, though when it's that hot.

Being an officer is a lot of responsibility. My stomach churns sometimes when I think about all the soldiers who are depending on me, a lot of them with their lives. So here's my average day: get up at 545 and get ready for work. At work by 0700. I get a brief from my soldier, Shelton, because he's on the night shift. I make my Daily Battle Update Brief slides on PowerPoint and then I give a brief to the Colonel around 0900. After that, I normally go on a little recon mission to meet other intel officers/soldiers who might be able to hook me up w/maps and other stuff sometime during the day. When my shift ends, my friend and I go over to the gym to work out. Then I go to bed and do it all over again.

I sure look forward to your letters and care packages. Keep 'em coming!

Love, Darcy


September 25


Hello Darcy,

How are you? Hope you're well and that this package finds you in good spirits. Lots of little goodies for you to eat, and be sure to look for your little bug—you'll know the significance once you watch the movie that's included, Under the Tuscan Sun. Couldn't stand the idea of your water not being good to drink, so you are now the proud owner of a Brita water pitcher with some extra filters. This package was fun to shop for. I just went from store to store, thinking of special things to make your work area beautiful (or the place you're living), and fun things to make you laugh and shake your head at that crazy mom of yours. Bekah sends the pound of Starbucks coffee.

I'm harvesting all kinds of things in the garden. The strawberries are gone now, but they were luscious. Hubbard squash are getting bigger by the day, and there's enough kale for us and the deer.

Thank you for opening up your heart wide to me, sweet daughter. I love you so much and miss you like crazy. Can't wait to see you again when your duty is over and you're back.

Love, Mom

November 12

Hey Mom,

Yeah, I know I haven't written for a while. Thought I'd better drop you a note to let you know I'm okay and everything's fine over here. I don't have a classified computer to work on right now, so this is the perfect time to write an email to you. I got the coffee Bekah sent. One of the biggest things we miss here is Starbucks. Real coffee is a good for bartering, too. Oh! I meant to tell you last time that the seeds and peat pots and potting soil were a big hit here. My *soldiers and I planted our seeds and watered them regularly, and we were so excited to see them sprout. But, unfortunately, we got too impatient and thought it would hurry things along if we put the pots out in the sun for a while, rather than on the high window sills that don't get much sun. Burned them all to hell. Oh well, it was really fun while it lasted.*

*Thanks for the email on Veterans Day. I really enjoyed the story about Grandpa Joe in combat. I feel like we are really doing something here, if not my unit, because we're just a signal unit, at least we are supporting the infantry men who are making things happen over here. They are doing dismounted patrols in city streets where just two days ago one of our soldiers was killed. It's tough when it's someone you know or have eaten chow with just the day before.*

*Anyway, love you and miss you.*

*xo Darcy*

After two tours of duty in the Middle East, Darcy served out her commitment to the military without incident and came back to Texas. On her birthday, Jane called.

"Happy birthday, honey!" She sat comfortably in the quiet living room with a glass of iced tea.

"Thanks, Mom. Thanks for the gift. It's just what I wanted. How did you know?"

"I had help from Bekah."

Darcy laughed. "Yeah, she would know."

Darcy was quiet a moment, then said, "Mom? I'm struggling with something and I could use some advice."

"What is it?" Jane asked.

"Well, you know I'm about to the end of my service in the military now. And because I'm a captain and they need officers, I'm being offered a signing bonus that is really tempting me to stay in."

Jane tried to see the situation from her young daughter's perspective: she'd had some frustrations, but also some success in the military. Although Darcy wouldn't say she flourished during her time serving her country, she did excel at what she did. She had come back from overseas with enough saved to put down on a beautiful new house. And now she was being offered both job security and more money, enough possibly, to make her life quite comfortable.

Jane swirled the tea in her glass as she put her thoughts together. "So were you considering staying in before they offered the signing bonus?"

"No. Not really. Dad says he thinks I should, but I don't know. It's the only job I've ever had. I like the structure of the military, you always know what you're supposed to be doing, you know the hierarchy, the routine. But I definitely don't like the bureaucracy. There's not much room for you to explore what you want to do, because you have to do what they want you to do."

"Well, I can't make the decision for you, but I can tell you this . . ."

Jane paused and let her gaze travel along the bookshelves against the wall. All the knowledge these books held, the wisdom of the great writers. She felt lacking by comparison. It suddenly struck her that wise or not, this was her chance to be a mother to Darcy. She had so much to offer her daughter from her experience and perspective.

"At the end of your life, is this career what you want to look back on as your contribution to the world? Is this what you want your life to stand for?"

Darcy was quiet.

"Because in the end, that's what it boils down to. Where your gifts and skills can take you and how you want to impact the world with your moment on the stage. Do you like being in the Army so much that you can see yourself waking up every morning of your life looking forward to going to work?"

"Well, no. But lots of people can say they don't wake up everyday rarin' to go to work. Look at Dad. He gets headaches on Saturday night before church service the next day."

"It's true that lots of people don't enjoy what they do. So do you want to be one of them? Or would you rather be part of those who love their careers?"

"Do you love being a teacher?" Darcy asked.

"I didn't say that so I could hold myself up to you. But I do. I love teaching the kids in my classroom. Bo says I have teaching in my blood. And I tell him he's a teacher to the bone. We were both meant to teach. Even with the headaches of dealing with the administration, I love walking into the classroom every day."

"But they're offering me a lot of money," Darcy said.

"Of course! They're trying to seduce you into staying. They know that most officers are smart enough to make it on the outside, and they want you to be dazzled by the money. They don't want you to think about what your other options are.

"If you could do anything you wanted, what would you choose, out of all the career choices in the world?"

Darcy was silent. In a moment, she said, "I'd go back to school and get my advanced degree in linguistics. I love linguistics. And I'm really good at it. I could see myself excited to go to work every day if I had that kind of job."

"Well, my dear," Jane said, "you are completely in charge of your destiny, whatever you can conceive it to be."

"Thanks, Mom. I appreciate your advice."

"Anytime, hon."

After Jane hung up, she clasped her hands together. Of course she would support her daughter's choice, whatever it might be. While she was ecstatic at being asked for advice, she was worried not knowing the outcome of their conversation. If Darcy should choose two more years in the Army in a combat zone, Jane didn't know if she could take it. The daily gnawing fear that something could happen to her in Afghanistan made her feel sick. She sipped her tea and put her feet on the coffee table.

Bo rounded the corner and came into the living room with the sports page. "What's up?"

Jane answered slowly. "I'm worried about Darcy."

"What's up with Captain D?"

Jane roused herself from her thoughts. "I'm scared. The Army is trying to seduce officers into re-upping by offering big bucks. She's considering it. If I hadn't called to wish her happy birthday when I did . . . She asked for some advice and I gave her some, but who knows?"

"Who knows what?"

"Who knows which way she'll go? She asked for some input. She's trying to decide whether to stay in or get out, now that her obligation's met. I basically helped her see the bigger picture, how she has the ultimate control of choosing what she wants to do with her life."

Bo nodded.

"We talked about her love of linguistics. So now she's considering going back to school. God, I hope she goes."

"She has the benefit of your advice to counter the idea put out by the military. Big bucks in trade for the possibility of losing your life is a lousy choice." He sat next to Jane and put an arm around her shoulder. "Still, hard to sit and wait for her to make her decision."

✍

As had become their tradition on Fridays after school, Jane and Bo went to their favorite restaurant. When the hostess called "Mr. and Mrs. Bernard," Jane smiled. He smiled back, looking pleased.

On the way to their table, Jane's phone rang. "It's Bekah," she said, foreboding in her voice.

Bo looked at her askance, then nodded. "I'll order the wine."

Jane shrugged as if to say, *Of course Bekah would call now—right on cue.* "I'll take it outside and be right back."

"Hello, Mom," Bekah said. "How are you?"

"Fine, honey. Listen, Bo and I were just being seated at a restaurant, so I'll have to make this short. I can call you back later, if you want."

"No. This will be short." She paused. "Ian and I have a bit of a problem."

"Oh?"

"Yes, it seems the used car we bought to drive out to California from Minnesota was a lemon. It's completely crapped out on us."

Jane's heart sank. She knew what was coming. "It's only been a couple months. Have you had it checked out by a mechanic?"

"Yes, of course."

"And what did he say?"

"Blown head gasket."

"Is it expensive to fix?"

"He said for how old this car is, it wouldn't be worth it to fix it. We should just buy a new car."

Jane folded her arms and looked down at the parking lot. She waited for what she knew would come. She steeled herself for what she knew she had to do—and it scared her to death.

"So we were wondering if you could cosign on a loan for a used car we're looking at."

Jane said quietly, "No, honey. I'm sorry, but I can't do that."

"What do you mean? You won't cosign with me?" Bekah said, voice full of shock and disappointment.

"No, I can't."

"Why not?"

"Do you remember the last time Bo and I cosigned for your car loan? Do you remember what happened when the loan was not quite paid off?"

"You mean you're not going to sign because we left the car in Minnesota?"

"No, it's because you left us holding the bag for your loan. To protect our credit, we paid the last three payments on your car loan."

Bekah was silent for a long moment. "I'm really sorry about that. But there was really no way we could afford to pay off that car and buy another one."

Jane sighed.

"I didn't know you'd be so bitter about it."

"Oh no, honey. I'm not bitter. I was never angry about it. It's just that I tried to help you see there would be consequences for your actions, and you chose to ignore that. So now you need to rebuild my trust in you."

"Okay, I get that. I can work on it. But you're really not going to help me?"

"Bekah, I love you so much, but I can't enable you to be irresponsible about money—especially when it comes to a credit rating. I would be the worst kind of parent if I did that."

There was a long pause. Jane's heartbeat sped up, her stomach churned.

"Well, you're not the only parent. I guess I've got to grovel to Dad."

Jane felt panicky and unsure of her firm stance only a moment before. Her worst fear was that the new bond between her and her daughter was not strong enough to hold. She dreaded the possibility of Bekah turning to her father, who would point out what a horrible mother Jane was after all—and wasn't she sorry now that she'd let Jane back into her life?

"What about Ian's parents?" Jane said, knowing that for Ian's parents, who were divorced and both worked in retail, it would be a huge stretch. But she could not help herself. She wanted Bekah to turn to anyone but Logan.

"Neither of them are able to help. They're both just barely making it."

It was silent a few moments longer, then Bekah said, "Alright. Well good-bye."

"Good-bye," Jane whispered, and hung up.

She walked back into the restaurant and sat down at the table where Bo waited. She glanced at his glass and realized he had a substantial lead.

He looked at her quizzically. "Well? What's new with Bekah?"

Jane smiled, shook her head. "I'll tell you all about it. But first, fill my wineglass, please."

# 14

While Jane cooked breakfast the next morning, she received a text from Darcy.

*Hey, Mom! Just wanted to let you know I've enrolled in a Ph.D. program in linguistics at UT Austin! I'm accepted for the summer quarter!*

Jane texted back, *Woo hoo! I'm so proud of you going after your goal!*

She was overjoyed and frustrated. Why couldn't Darcy phone her with the good news? She sighed, thankful that Bekah had long ago made her aware that texting was simply a generational difference.

She wondered when she would hear from Bekah again. She was afraid to call her. Afraid if she called, she would cave in and act like the Bank of Mom in order to block Logan's ability to help her out financially—and to weasel his way back into Bekah's life.

Over cups of hot coffee and omelets, Bolivar tried to ease her mind, saying that financial immaturity was rampant among young adults and asking for a rescue was simply what many in their twenties did to their parents. Besides, Logan didn't have that kind of power anymore.

Jane disagreed. She was culpable for her many financial rescues of Bekah in the past and knew it resulted in an irresistible pull on Bekah's character. Like flowing water seeking out the lowest pool, Bekah was drawn toward reckless financial behavior. Living beyond her means would become self-destructive if it continued. No matter how painful it was to Bekah, Jane was determined to guide her daughter toward becoming a wise and financially mature adult.

Hunching his shoulders, Bo's hands around his cup, he said, "You're right. Knowing that rat, he may try. But Bekah loves you and she's not going to be fooled twice."

Later, Jane heard the dim racket of the tiller's engine. Bo was in the garden plowing up the soil, plowing the weeds between the rows, turning the dense clay into loamy soil. They both viewed tending the garden as almost a holy activity, connecting them to each other and to the earth.

She stood at the window, her palm on the glass, watching Bo and she smiled.

One day in late summer, Bekah called.

"Big news, Mom! Ian and I are getting married."

"Oh, honey! I'm so happy for you!" The news made her glad, but she was overjoyed simply to hear her daughter's voice for the first time since she had refused to cosign for their car.

"Yeah, I'm in the clouds," Bekah said, happiness shining through her voice.

They would be getting married in the fall. It would be a wedding on the beach in Santa Cruz where they lived. She had already contacted a small, local art museum that had agreed to rent out the facility for the reception.

"How creative!" Jane said. "I would never have thought of an art museum for your reception."

"Yeah, they said this was their first wedding reception request. But they're small and their board decided it's as good a revenue stream as any."

"How much are they charging?" Jane asked.

"I don't know yet. They're supposed to get back to me." Bekah paused. "I've just sent you a picture of the wedding dress I want. Check your email."

Jane went to her computer and opened the email attachment. "It's gorgeous!" she said, and the chain reaction of thoughts that came with a daughter's announcement of her nuptials took place: dress, reception facility, catering, flowers. *How much? How much? How much?*

"Bo and I want to help, of course. Have you spoken to your father about helping?"

Bekah was silent a moment. "Yes. He didn't offer to help financially. He tried talking me out of marrying a heathen. Then, when I wouldn't budge, he said he wanted to do the ceremony. But when I told him we'd already arranged to be married by Ian's uncle, who got his nondenominational minister's license online, he got kinda chilly real quick."

"Oh. Well, I guess that would do it." Jane realized with a start that Bekah had shared her wedding announcement with her father before she had shared it with her.

"Yeah, I wanted to ask him first to help with the expenses, father of the bride and all. But after talking with him, we're not counting on much help there. So you and Bo can help?"

"Of course. We're happy to help. Let me know about what kind of budget you're looking at, and Bo and I will talk. Let me know how much your dress is, what the rental of the hall is. There's flowers, food. We can pick up some bottles of red and white wine at Trader Joe's. How many people?"

"We're trying to keep it small. Maybe 50?"

"Oh . . . That's quite a few." Fear flooded through Jane. If she and Bo were the main source of wedding funding, it could be a big hit. And even though Simon's and Darcy's work study programs helped, the ripples of wedding expenses would affect their ability to help with Simon's and Darcy's monthly support. Two kids in college and a wedding: the perfection of bad timing.

"Fifty is not a lot, compared to friends of mine. It's only 25 people for Ian and 25 for me."

"Okay. I'll talk to Bo."

"Thanks, Mom." Bekah brightened. "I need to get my dress ordered and the invitations fairly soon. I'll email you an estimate."

"Sure. It's only a few months away. Better get crackin'! Oh, be sure to give me the date as soon as possible so I can order airline tickets. I'll need to let grandma and grandpa and Louise know, too."

The wedding dress was reasonable by wedding dress standards, only a thousand dollars, give or take some change. The deposit to hold the reception in the art museum was also reasonable, as was the insurance they took out to cover any damages to the place, as required. The items chosen from the catering menu were reasonable as well, but times 50 people made Jane and Bolivar begin to sweat. Jane asked if they could use seaweed instead of flowers, since the ceremony would take place on the beach. Bekah was not amused, but she did cut back her original vision of how the beach would be decorated. It didn't help that the city of Santa Cruz surprised them with a hefty fee for weddings held on the beach. But the surprise bill from the city was just a small blip in the wedding expenses tally. Bekah and Ian had no budget to speak of, and with no help from the father of the bride or the parents of the groom, the expenses were mounting fast and outstripping the budget Jane and Bo had put together.

"We can't absorb much more," Bolivar said, taking the hoe to the garden soil. "We've got Simon to think of. Darcy now, too. They're both taking summer classes and need our help. Having two kids in college is no picnic."

"I know. It's just—" Jane wiped the sweat from her brow and replaced her straw hat. "You don't know how hard it is to keep telling Bekah she needs to downsize and downsize some more."

Bo chopped at weeds with the hoe, and Jane knelt while she pulled weeds from between the cucumber plants. She and Bo had come out to the garden when it was cool in the early morning, and they were almost finished weeding. The sun was high in the sky.

"She's got how many on her guest list now?" Bo asked.

"Down from 50 to 35. She's ready to order the invitations, I think."

"Didn't we talk about cutting her guest list in half?" Bo stopped his work, hoe in hand, and wiped at his forehead with his sleeve. "The number of people coming makes it impossible."

Jane kept her eyes on the ground, digging with a claw-shaped tool. "Maybe you should talk to her."

"Jane." He was silent, looking off over the tops of the walnut tree at the far side of the garden. He seemed to gather his thoughts, his gaze settling on a portion of the garden, lush and green, pay-off for their hard work: green beans, the giant leaves of squash, strawberries, raspberries, zucchini, tomatoes, cucumbers, the corn stalks straight and tall. "We agreed we didn't want to go into debt for this wedding. She has to work with what we've got and commitments we've already made to Simon and Darcy. What if a medical emergency comes up and we've drained our savings or put it all on our credit card so she could have a nice party?"

"It's not a party. It's a wedding and reception."

"You've got to tell her. She can't have more than 25 guests. That's a dozen fam and friends for each of 'em. That's going to have to do it."

Jane shielded her eyes and looked up at Bo. The sun shone in a bright outline around him. She knew he took their commitment to helping put two children through college seriously.

"All right. I'll tell her." She stood up, brushed off her knees, and pulled off her garden gloves. "I'd better go now, before she places her order for the invitations."

But when Jane called Bekah, she found that the order had already been placed and it was too late to cancel. Jane sighed. "Well, nothing we can do now. We'll eat the extra expense of the invitations, but you've got to whittle down the guest list to 25. That's all we can afford right now, since we have obligations to Darcy and Simon."

"Okay, Mom," Bekah said, her voice calm. It was as if she had decided before the phone call that anything her mother said, she would accept. Jane didn't quite know how to take it.

"I'm sorry, honey. I wish we could do more to help. It's just impossible to stretch our money any further. Bad timing with Darcy and Simon in school."

"I understand," Bekah said, voice full of understanding. "Ian and I are the ones who decided we wanted to get married now, not wait. We are very grateful for any help you and Bo can give to us. I won't lie—we've had a fight or two about cutting down the guest list. But like I said, we are very grateful for you pitching in to help us. Fighting or not, I don't think I'll be divorced before I'm married."

"Maybe you should think about making the reception a potluck. I think our family and his and your closest friends would love to bring their favorite dishes."

Bekah's voice was serene. "I'll talk to him about it. We'll go at it again to trim the list to twenty-five. We can be happy just having family there, if it comes to that."

Bekah was being uncharacteristically philosophical, mature. Still, disappointment ate at Jane's stomach. The happiness of planning with her daughter for her wedding was fast being replaced by worry that she would be seen as stingy and the cause of wrecked dreams of the perfect wedding. "If you want to put off the ceremony until you and Ian have had a chance to save up . . ."

"No, no, we'll work within your budget," she said. "We're lucky to have your help. Dad is being a perfect ass. When I called the other day to ask him for grandpa Churlick's address, he wouldn't give it to me."

"Aw, honey."

After a thoughtful pause, Bekah said, "So there's two we can take off the guest list." Then she added, "Maybe four."

# 15

A couple of days later, Logan Churlick screamed at Jane, "I know you put her up to this!"

The volume of the phone call was like a punch in the face. She held the cell phone out from her ear. It took her a moment to respond. "What are you talking about?"

"You know exactly what I'm talking about, you b—" But he did not say the word, because swearing was against his morality.

"I have no idea what you're talking about," Jane said, and then it occurred to her what was behind his rage: no invitation to Bekah's wedding.

"I swear, I will make you pay for this humiliation," Logan hissed.

"Have you talked to Bekah about it?"

"You. You're the one who gave her the idea. Probably to pay me back for not paying for any of her wedding. But she's marrying a heathen, and I cannot support that. You were the one who was always stingy. You and your whole family are stingy. But this is just plain cruel. I don't deserve this kind of disrespect."

His rambling was hard for her to follow.

"Stingy? Bo and I are helping Bekah out with the wedding expenses. How much have you chipped in?"

"See? Using that against me. First, you got her to have someone else do the ceremony and now this. I didn't know you could sink so low. But I swear, Jane, you're going to pay for this. I'm going to do everything in my power to bring you down. You and your family. The gloves are off." He screamed, "Do you hear me? I will crush you!"

Jane held her phone out from her ear and pushed the button to disconnect.

That afternoon, she walked down to the row of mailboxes on the street and picked up their mail. She noticed an envelope holding Bekah's wedding invitation and thought of Logan.

Jane walked into the cool kitchen waving the envelope. "Wedding bells!"

Bo turned from the sink where he was dipping something into a measuring cup filled with a vile-smelling liquid. He smiled. "Glad to see we've got something tangible out of our donations to this blessed event."

"What are you doing with my measuring cup?"

"Fixing the mower," he said, dipping the greasy item into the cup.

"Guess I'm donating that one to the garage." She ran her finger under the envelope flap and pulled out the invitation. It was heavy stock with script on the front, ocean and sand behind the words.

"Oh, my God, Bo! So this is what he was talking about."

"What? Who?"

Jane raised her head from the invitation, eyes wide. She held up the invitation. "Logan called earlier today. You were out, so I haven't told you about it yet. He. Was.

*Pissed.* Now I know why. It says here that Bekah Bernard and Ian Grant are getting married."

Bo looked at her quizzically. "What's going on? Why is she using Bernard rather than Churlick?"

"I don't know, but I'm going to find out," Jane said, retrieving her cell phone from her purse.

Bekah did not answer her phone, so Jane left a message. Then she filled Bolivar in on Logan's call.

Bo whistled. "I'll *bet* he was pissed, in a passing-a-kidney-stone kind of way." He turned back to the sink, dipped the widget into the measuring cup, and shook his head. "And so, of course, you're to blame."

"Yup. The girls can't do anything unless I'm manipulating them to do it."

"They basically have no brain stems," Bo said.

Jane's smile turned into a frown. "I'm worried about the wedding. You didn't hear him screaming at me on the phone like a maniac. It looks like Bekah, in her wisdom, sent him an invitation to twist the knife, since he refused to help pay for the wedding. So then he refused to give her his parents' address so she could invite them. But now he knows when and where the wedding is taking place."

A week later, Simon called.

"Hey, how's it going?" Bo said.

"Pretty good. I've got a little problem, though, and I need your help."

"Shoot."

"Well, this course I'm taking has lab fees and it requires a huge text book, written by the instructor of course. It's really expensive. But I don't have money for the lab or the book."

"No problem, son. I'll write you a check and get it in today's mail. Is that okay?"

"Well, no. I needed it yesterday, actually. Can you give me your credit card number?"

"I don't think you can sign for my credit card, Simon. But I'll tell you what. You give me the name of the text and the number of the campus bookstore and the number of whoever I have to pay for the lab, and I'll do it all with my credit card over the phone."

"Sounds good, Dad. I'll text you the information. Thanks!"

But Bolivar was not able to charge the textbook or lab fee.

"Jane, do you know what's going on with our credit card? I called to see why I can't pay for Simon's school costs and they say it's maxed out."

She looked up at him from the kitchen table filled with wedding favors she was working on. "Really? Oh no. It sounds like a perfect storm."

"What do you mean?"

Jane's eyes went to the ceiling and she ticked off a dizzying list of expenses for the month. "We just got our monthly credit card statement. Remember that car repair? And then there's Simon's and Darcy's tuition for summer classes. I couldn't wait any longer to buy our airline tickets for flying down to Santa Cruz. And don't forget, we're getting Simon's and Darcy's tickets, too, since they can't afford it. The wedding gift could've waited till next month, I guess. And, of course, the never-ending wedding expenses. I just didn't think about it all hitting at once."

Bolivar ran his hand absently over the weekend stubble on his chin. "So how am I supposed to help Simon with what he needs at the university?"

"Oh! I'm so sorry, honey."

Bo inhaled deeply. "You're sorry. What do I tell Simon?"

Jane and Bolivar had rarely fought over money. But the tension and resentment of the past couple months' spending was there, under the surface, ready to be ignited by a well-timed financial emergency.

"What do you think? Shall I tell Simon to drop out?"

Jane's stomach lurched and she couldn't tell if he was trying to be funny. "No. Not at all. I-I said I was sorry. What else can I do?"

"Nothing. I don't know what we can do. I guess we can get a cash advance on our credit card. Expensive, but we don't have much choice."

Jane nodded.

We're both going to have to cut corners for a while. Okay?"

She said nothing, but nodded again.

A week went by before Jane heard from Bekah, but the residue from the scene with Bolivar still rankled.

"Hi, Mom. Sorry it took me a while to get back to you. It's been crazy busy here. Only a month to go, you know."

"Yes, I know. Only a month."

"Amen and hallelujah, right?"

Jane was struck by her daughter's equanimity. How had her Bekah grown up so fast, considering the insecurity and hair-triggered temper she had brought with her from

Rathcreek? "Just tell me you don't have any unexpected expenses."

"Don't worry, Mom. No surprises this phone call."

"Sorry, honey. I've been a little uptight lately. But I do have a question: what's behind listing your name as Bekah Bernard, rather than Churlick, on the wedding invitations?"

"I can't tell you. I want to tell you in person."

"Why?"

"I just told you—no surprises this phone call," Bekah said. "I'll reveal the entire mystery later."

Worry wormed its way through Jane, and she felt not like someone who was helping her daughter orchestrate her wedding, but rather like an outsider who had to wait for explanations that couldn't be given over the phone. She said, "Well, you can probably imagine your dad's reaction."

"Yeah. He's probably pretty pissed. But honestly? I don't care."

"He called and read me the riot act."

"Sounds like something he'd do." Then, a fury held in for too long broke loose. "He thinks he can just do anything he wants to me and Darcy. He's refused to give me my Grandpa's address so I could invite him to the wedding. Asshole! Father of the bride and he's not willing to pay one cent for my wedding or do anything to help Darcy with her education.

"And don't forget, when I asked for an apology about turning me and Darcy against you when we were little, they have never so much as said they were responsible for *any*thing, let alone say they were sorry. Darcy and I were orphaned by you. Not that I blame you. I blame them. The crap they fed us turned us into little monsters. And we were too young to question it. So the least of my concerns is what he thinks about my wedding invitation. Screw him! Screw them both!"

Bekah's words stunned Jane. Conflicting emotions crashed through her. She was overjoyed that Bekah saw her father for who he truly was. Vindication flooded her senses like a sweet intoxicant that obliterated years of suffering and doubt about her own place in her daughter's heart. At the same time, she was seized with fear for Bekah; she despaired over the acrimony she heard in her daughter's voice. Where was her sweet daughter? The truth she had finally grasped seemed to be eating her from the inside, like a snake eating its own tail until it devours itself.

*God, it's like looking into a mirror. She's going through it just like I did. It took me time to get over that man's manipulation and lies. Maybe with time, she'll get over it, too.*

She said, "We'll have to talk someday about how to let go of that anger."

"I don't *want* to let go of it!"

Jane was silent a moment, unsure of how to proceed. She decided to steer clear, saving it for another day. "I'm not as concerned about your hurting Logan's feelings as much as I'm worried about what he might do to ruin your wedding day."

"Do you think he would do something?"

"He was very angry."

"Hmm. I should've thought this through a little better, I guess."

Jane said, "Ya think?" And she could tell from the giggling on the other end of the phone that Bekah would be all right.

"Well, it's done now," Bekah said. "If something comes up at the wedding, we'll deal with it.

"There's probably only one thing I could do to burn his ass more, and I've just done it. I phoned Bo before I called you, and asked him to walk me down the aisle. He said yes."

# 16

Bekah's wedding day arrived with a rosy sunrise, an early morning marine layer that was forecast to give way to sun, a slight breeze, and 70 degrees.

By nine o'clock in the morning, the beach was bedecked by the wedding party of Bekah's and Ian's friends with fronds of pampas grass, illegally plucked and transplanted, much to Jane's dismay. But the deed was done and she begrudgingly admitted that despite the harm to the ecosystem, it looked beautiful. The tall and stately pampas outlined the aisle Bekah and Bo would walk down to where the minister would stand, his back to the ocean.

Their friends scurried up and down the stairway to bring down folding chairs they placed on the sand creating an aisle between them. People watched from the railing on the cliff above as the bridesmaids, hair in curlers, and groomsmen in cut-offs, put the final touches in place before leaving to get themselves ready for the ceremony.

Waves lapped languorously at the shore. Bekah, Jane, Bo, Simon, and Darcy stood high above the water on the cliff overlooking the sea below. The bright midmorning sun sparkled off the tiny jewels of the lacy bridal gown. Bekah's hair was arranged in such a way that she looked somehow more mature than her twenty-one years. The vision of loveliness, so incongruous to her usual bad ass self, was set off by pink hair and sundry tattoos on her arms. These touches of genuine Bekah were complimented by the radiant happiness of a woman about to marry.

She kissed Jane's cheek and hugged her.

Darcy, maid of honor in a blue blush of chiffon, kissed Jane's other cheek. Simon, wearing a suit, stood nearby.

Bo watched Jane with her girls, and beaming, said, "Better be careful, or all the care going into your makeup will be undone."

"Waterproof." Bekah smiled and blinked back tears. "I love you both so much. Thank you for making this possible," she said in a quiet voice. "I have something important to tell you both, now that I have you together."

Jane and Bolivar looked at each other. Jane's long chestnut hair shone in the sunlight, copper highlights glinting in a ring at her crown. The sun shone on the ruby hair ornaments that seemed consecrated to her beauty, innate confidence, and serene happiness. The deep rose-colored dress that Bekah had insisted was perfect, hugged her mother from the wide v-neck to mid-calf above delicate sandals that strapped her ankles. But it was her eyes, filled with love and tenderness for her daughter, in fact, for all the world on this day, that set her apart from everyone else.

Bolivar patted Bekah's arm that was hooked with his. Standing tall in a tan suit, white shirt, and tie, he drew his

wife to him with his other arm and kissed her hair. Then
he pulled Darcy into the circle of love and squeezed her
shoulders. "We're all here. What's so important?"

Bekah took a deep breath, let it out slowly. "Okay,
well, you know about the invitations with my last name
as Bernard."

They nodded.

Bekah seemed choked up for a moment, then choosing
her words carefully, said, "My name was on the invitations
that way because Bekah Bernard is my legal name."

Bo and Jane stared at her, then each other, trying to
make sense of the revelation.

"When Ian and I first talked about getting married,
he asked if I was going to change my name. That got me
thinking. I thought long and hard about everything we've
been through together, as a family, how grateful I am that
you accepted me into your home and hearts when I was
at the lowest I've ever been: I was in total rebellion in
Rathcreek, an embarrassment and failure to my so-called
parents. I don't know if you really understand how, even
though I was so bad-ass, I was scared shitless, given all I'd
been told my whole life by my dad.

"I mean, I was going straight to hell. You made all that
go away. You helped me to see that Rathcreek was one little
set of rules that ran my world, but there was a whole lot
of rules outside of Rathcreek, outside my father's beliefs,
to choose from."

Jane's joy was only overtaken by her pride. "You've
made more progress than you can see, Bekah. Remember
how you were when you first came to live with us?"

"Maybe. Yeah, I guess so, now that I think about it. All
I know is it's such a relief to know I don't have to judge

everyone and belong to his exclusive little club to feel safe. Ha! All I ever felt was scared." She shook her head. "Yeah, I've made progress, but I'll never be able to give everyone the benefit of the doubt like you do, Mom."

Bekah took Bo's and Jane's hands in her own.

"So the reason things were so tight for Ian and me during all the wedding plans? I went to a lawyer who negotiated the very costly, complicated task of *reversing* my legal adoption by Dolores and while we were at it, changing my last name to yours and Bo's. It's so important to me that things are back the way they should have always been."

Jane gasped, hand to her mouth, undone by the shock and happiness flooding through her. Bekah hugged her, tears spilling from bright green eyes.

"You're legally my mom again. You'll always be my mom—you and no one else. And Bo, you've always been the dad who believed in me and loved me unconditionally. Now I'm legally a Bernard."

Bekah hugged Bolivar, who wiped at his eyes.

Jane let out a cry of delight. "Bekah Bernard! I am overflowing." She tightened her embrace. All of her worry, pointless. The months of anxiety, imagining her angry daughter taking up with Logan, who would waste no time in turning her against her mother in a déjà vu of the horror she and her daughters had barely survived—pointless. Bekah could be angry, as all children were with their parents from time to time, and not cut her mother out of her life. Sweet, overflowing relief and love filled Jane's heart.

Darcy cried, "I want credit. This is one time I didn't let the cat out of the bag, Bekah!" She looked from her twin to her mother, to Bo and Simon. "Bekah and I had a lot of phone conversations about this while I was at school. We are in absolute agreement that although he may be our father, we will resist any of his attempts to take us back to his dark view of you. We will never ever buy his view of the world again. It was a hard lesson, but we've seen the light."

"Darcy," Jane murmured, hugging her daughter. "Overflowing."

Simon raised his hand. "Way to go, sis!"

Bekah gave him a high five.

Strains of music played below on the beach. Bekah, Darcy, and their parents stayed locked in their embrace until the best man, who stood waiting to walk the mother of the bride down the stairs, tugged gently at Jane's arm. She quickly drew a tissue from her purse and dabbed at Bekah's makeup, Darcy's, then her own.

"You've made me very happy, my daughters," Jane said, voice thick with emotion.

She let herself be led down the stairs on the arm of Ian's best man. Darcy, the only bridesmaid, waited a few moments, then with Simon at her side, followed Jane down the stairway to the beach.

Bo said, "And as for me, Bekah Bernard, at least for another thirty minutes or so until you become Mrs. Ian Grant, I am absolutely the proudest father of the bride in the history of the institution of fathers of brides."

Looking at the sea, as if she were trying to avoid fresh tears, Bekah stared straight ahead and said, "I didn't know how a normal father should be. Now I do. You are absolutely the best dad I could ever hope for. And that's why Ian agreed with my decision to keep my maiden name."

❧

Bo and Bekah descended the stairs from the cliff. People unknown to them gawked, hanging over the cliff's railing. The small group of people beloved by them below on the beach stood to the music declaring the bride had appeared.

Bekah began her descent on her father's arm unaware that far below on the sand, a commotion was taking place. Guests watched as Ian's Uncle Beck, readying to perform the ceremony, struggled to maintain his place at the head of the assemblage. Eventually, after a struggle of wills, Ian's uncle meekly stood aside. Logan Churlick, clad in black suit, white shirt, and tie, stood next to the groom, who frowned, shaking his head. Logan faced those assembled with a bible in his hand.

Bekah and Bo ambled across the sand, through the pampas grass aisle, and stopped when they reached Logan. Bekah's face, for all her serenity and beauty of just minutes before, held a look equal parts fury and embarrassment.

Bo gently transferred his daughter to her husband to be, then said to Logan, "You've got exactly ten seconds to get your ass out of here."

Churlick, eyes bright with disdain, stood momentarily paralyzed, then, as if switched on, came to life. "We've prayed about it and we've forgiven Janey for turning our daughters against us."

Bolivar's arm came back, fist doubled.

The guests breathed in a collective gasp, then there was stunned silence.

Jane let loose an ear-shattering scream. The sound averted what would surely have been the beginning of a brawl. She did not want her daughter's wedding to deteriorate into a fracas.

Jane rushed forward from her seat, graceless in the sand, and stood facing Churlick.

"You are not welcome at this ceremony, and you're certainly not performing it."

"I have a right, as her father—"

"And her mother!" Dolores shrieked from her seat along the edge of the pampas grass.

"No! You don't have any right to *anything* to do with me ever again," Bekah yelled. "I can't even believe you two are here. Such fucking assholes."

Jane trembled with fury. She willed her voice not to shake. "You heard her. Now get out of here."

Bolivar said ominously, fist tightened, "On your own two feet or not, it's no difference to me."

Churlick's voice was choked with anger. "I know what's behind—"

"No, you don't!" Jane shouted. "This is *Bekah's* day. Not yours. Now you two, get the hell out of here."

"We're not going anywhere." He glared at Bekah. "If you'll recall, Bekah *Bernard*, we were invited."

Darcy, usually a mild follower of her twin sister, stepped beside her mother. "Well, Bekah and I are *uninviting* you to this wedding right here and right now!"

Churlick froze, turning his gaze on his daughters, who until then, he had not even looked at. "I'm your father, young lady, and if you think—"

Bekah stepped forward. "You may have fathered us, but you are *not* our father! We're not only uninviting you to my wedding, but Darcy and I are uninviting you to our lives. You are no father to me."

"Or to me!" Darcy cried.

The wedding guests stirred in their seats, murmuring, transfixed.

Jane jabbed a finger at Churlick, radiating fury. "You never showed Bekah and Darcy the kind of love a real father has. To you, they were *two souls to be brought to Jesus.* Listen to her now, Logan. She's rejecting you and your Nazi god."

Bekah held herself erect. "And don't forget Satan. I was scared to death of Satan. That's what I remember. And I remember many, many smears against my mother. You took my mother from me!"

"I was simply taking care of your soul," Churlick hissed. "You'd choose her over heaven? How can you reject eternal life in heaven?"

"Fuck your heaven. I reject you and your self-righteous arrogance. And I reject your arrogant grab to ruin my wedding day."

Darcy, chin held high, spoke up. "We will always resist everything you and Dolores stand for."

A wail came from the chairs. "Sugar bear!" Dolores' open mouth was a cavern of grief. Mascara slid down her cheeks in a cascade of tears.

Nearby, Louise stood and cupped her hands around her mouth. "Can it, *Mommy Dearest!* A real mother wouldn't fill these girls' minds full of sewage about their sweet mother . . . year after year—after *fuckin' year!*"

The merciless sun beat down upon them. Churlick's brow was beaded with sweat. He ran his hand through graying hair, looking from Louise to his wife to Jane and her daughters. A gull screamed overhead as it soared through the solid blue toward the horizon.

Churlick glared at Jane. "I didn't take your mother from you. Your *real* mother gave you up. Gave up her own flesh and blood." He looked through narrowed eyes at Bekah, who stared back in defiance. "Of course she'd put you up to defending her."

Guilt shot through Jane and she flinched. As always, he hit the target he knew would take her down. Misery sat heavy in her gut.

"My mother may not be perfect, but she loves me with everything in her. And Bo loves me. He treats me more like a dad than you ever did."

"But *I* am your father. What's more, someday, I'll be your children's grandfather. And don't think for a moment I won't exercise my rights to teach them about the all-powerful, all-knowing God in heaven."

Bekah screamed, "No! There's no fucking way you're going to do to them what you did to Darcy and me."

"I can't believe this," Darcy said. "It's like déjà vu."

"You are no father to us," Bekah said. She called to Dolores, "And you are no mother."

Dolores broke down and wept disconsolately. Logan's shoulders sagged. His face was haggard and he could not speak. He could not look at his daughters.

When Bekah saw this, her tone changed. A complexity of emotions, far beyond anger, far beyond her years, crept into her eyes. Her voice was tinged with sadness. "I don't know if you even *can* love. The only thing you care about is yourself—and the deity you manufactured to beat Darcy and me into submission. Pathetic. But I'll tell you this: you have earned the consequences of your actions. What you did all those years ago, and are still doing today, is so deplorable it makes me sick to my stomach."

Jane stared at Bekah, overcome. *My God, she gets it. She's risen above the anger. She sees that the father she thought was some sort of holy mouthpiece of God is just a man.*

Logan's eyes connected with Jane's. She watched the shock roll through him. He had lost everything that meant anything to him. Lost the only love he'd ever wanted when Jane spurned him years ago, and now was facing the loss of his daughters. He looked like a cornered animal trying to see a way to translate what was happening into his own fanatical view of reality.

Logan drew air through quivering lips, then, with a new-found momentum, he spat, "This isn't real. Couldn't be. You've been brainwashed by that *bitch* you call Mom."

Bolivar, gathering his rage into a fist, launched it into Logan Churlick's chin. Legs came out from under Logan, spewing sand, and he flew three feet backward, landing with a thud.

Dolores screamed, a hand to her chest. A ripple of gasps went through those seated.

Jane's father came forward and nodded at the crumpled form sprawled on the sand. "Let's get this sorry excuse for a human being off the beach."

Bolivar nodded and grabbed Churlick under one arm while Joe Crownhart grabbed him under the other.

Shaking his head as if to clear it, Logan slumped as they dragged him down the aisle of pampas grass.

Dolores stood and shrieked, "I hope you heathens burn in hell!"

"Bringing up the rear with Monster Mommy, tra la, tra la!" Louise said, and pushed Dolores ahead of her. They followed the men toward the stairway that led up to the cliff.

Up above, the crowd was leaning over the railing at the cliff's edge.

When Bo, Joe, and Louise returned, they took their seats. A mild breeze blew in from the sea, the air was expectant. Everyone was silent as Ian's Uncle Beck cleared his throat and assumed his place before Bekah and Ian.

"Dearly beloved, it's not often I get to officiate at a wedding. But a wedding and the pugilistic vanquish of evil—all in one day!" He chuckled.

A nervous titter ran through the guests.

"Seriously, folks. A disaster was averted. Lives that were disasters have been made whole. Made whole by loving parents who stood by these daughters. You don't see that kind of thing every day. Sometimes you don't see it in a lifetime."

Uncle Beck beamed. "Just wanted to point that out to you, as the adrenalin eases up a bit."

The sun shone upon Uncle Beck, Bekah and Ian, and their loved ones. Waves lapped the shore, in and out in the unending rhythm of an abundant sea that had ebbed and flowed for millennia.

Bo leaned over and whispered to Jane, "Something's always going to try to get in the way of love—sometimes it's ourselves. That's life. It's not always advisable to fight for love, but if there's no other way—"

Jane squeezed her husband's hand. "There's nothing more worth fighting for. Nothing is more important in this existence than love. It's worth dying for."

Uncle Beck said, "Ian, would you take the hand of your beautiful bride?"

After the wedding, when events had sunk in, Jane and Bo talked about the day.

Bo was Bekah's and Darcy's father. Bo, the dragon killer, had come through for them all. Jane's fear of ever losing her girls again had evaporated. Her worry over the depth and constancy of Bo's love vanished. Her residual guilt and the painful, biting hatred of Logan and Dolores Churlick were released. She was free.

On Monday morning, Jane stood in front of her senior English class. She smiled at her students, lighting up the room.

"Today we are going to discuss approaches to ending the stories you've been working on. There are several. There's the cliff hanger. The explicit ending. The twist ending. Unresolved ending.

"There's another one that is quite satisfying. Maybe not as far as literature goes, but many people would choose it, if they're honest. The HEA ending."

Her students looked at her quizzically.

"Happily ever after," she said.

# AUTHOR'S NOTE

I hope you have enjoyed reading *From Ice and Snow* and that your cravings to know how things turned out for me and my girls were satisfied after reading the foundation story, *The Protest*. On a personal note, I would like to say, *Thank you very much for taking the time to read my book.*

If you would like to know when I have a new book or short story coming out, you can sign up for the New Release Newsletter here (https://www.diannebunnell.com/). I will only send out an email when I have a new story out (about once a year) and I will always offer my new book at a steep discount to people on my New Release list. Also, I value your privacy and would never sell your email address to anyone.

# OTHER BOOKS
# BY
# DIANNE KOZDREY BUNNELL

*The Protest:* A fictional memoir inspired by the real-life religious hijacking of Dianne Kozdrey Bunnell's two daughters, ages 10 and 12 by fundamentalist Christianity gone awry. This book lays the foundation and is the precursor to *From Ice and Snow*, sequel to *The Protest.*

*The Protest: https://www.amazon.com/Protest-Fictional -Memoir-Life-Calling-ebook/dp/B00UW51OLW/*

*A Blue Moon Phase of the Heart:* coming soon

*The Inheritance:* A short story coming soon

## ACKNOWLEDGEMENTS

A work of literature is never truly written alone. We writers have the honor of putting thoughts, emotion, images, and words to page, but usually our writing colleagues, editors, and loved ones have contributed to a greater or lesser degree along the way. And to those special people, I owe a great debt.

Professionally, I have to say that this book would not be, if it weren't for the urging of my writing pals, Shawn Inmon and John Draper. It started out as part of a larger story, a tiny fraction of this final version. Shawn and John urged me to tell the story without abbreviation. The full-on telling resulted in *From Ice and Snow*. Thank you both for wisely advising me to explore the story in its entirety to produce a full-length sequel to *The Protest*. Thank you also for your excellent critiquing of each chapter as it came off the keyboard.

Thanks, also, to Irene Wanner, my editor. I appreciate your skill in seeing things that needed to be expanded, clarified, or for suggesting that a passage could be better written.

Last, I'd like to thank my husband Phil for his faith in my ability and for his insights into realistic characterizations and intriguing plot twists that added so much to the story. We never did agree on the Hitchcock ending, but it gave us the best inside joke that will continue to make us laugh through many years to come.

# ABOUT THE AUTHOR

Born in Michigan, I am the oldest of seven children. I moved with my family to California where I lived through my teen years, and then migrated to Washington state, where I've lived for over three decades.

I graduated magna cum laude from Whitworth University with a BA in English, which allowed me to pursue my dream of teaching high school English for several years. I love teaching and the craziness and fun that go into making reading and writing interesting to teens. In addition, before I began my teaching career, I have been an executive assistant to a U.S. Congressman, a hospital CEO, and confidential secretary to a two-year college president.

My first book, *The Protest*, will always have a special place in my heart. It took me ten years to write and probably saved my sanity when I lost my two daughters to a religious hijacking. My motive for writing the story? I was desperate to make something good out of the horrific situation that led to the loss of my girls. My thinking was: if only I could help others faced with similar situations, it would help me to survive as well. And that's exactly what happened.

CPSIA information can be obtained
at www.ICGtesting.com
Printed in the USA
LVOW11s0753190417
531359LV00002B/135/P